John lives near Calgary, Canada, with his wife of many happy years. Together they have raised four children to adulthood.

John and his wife met at a church in Edmonton and have since lived in several locations to follow his career. Included in their travels is a time in Scotland as volunteers in a Christian drug rehab program for young men.

A career in the Petroleum Industry as a tradesman, inspector supervisor, and consultant was paralleled by his involvement in Christian church activities including that of teacher, leader, board member, and Elder.

His keen interest in church affairs and his training in quality management has given him an understanding about how governance and theology should work together.

John is continually careful to rest his experience on what the Bible has to say about the state of the affairs of men's hearts and lives.

To the many pastors and teachers who have greatly enriched my life through their faithful ministry.

John Duncan

PEW TENDERS ARISE

A MANIFESTO OF FAITH

AUSTIN MACAULEY PUBLISHERS™

LONDON • CAMBRIDGE • NEW YORK • SHARJAH

Ordering Information:
Quantity sales: special discounts are available on quantity purchases by corporations, associations, and others. For details, contact the publisher at the address below.

Publisher's Cataloging-in-Publication data
Duncan, John
Pew Tenders Arise: A Manifesto of Faith

ISBN 9781643788203 (Paperback)
ISBN 9781643788210 (Hardback)
ISBN 9781645365280 (ePub e-book)

Library of Congress Control Number: 2019911797

The main category of the book — RELIGION / General

www.austinmacauley.com/us

First Published (2019)
Austin Macauley Publishers LLC
40 Wall Street, 28th Floor
New York, NY 10005
USA

mail-usa@austinmacauley.com
+1 (646) 5125767

"John B. Duncan's book, *Pew Tenders Arise*, is an antidote to the chaos of the present (church) Community of the Spirit. With precision and care, John breaks down many of the preconceptions and traditions of the Bride of Christ, while graciously reminding her of the foundations and directions of Christ laid out in the New Testament through the power of the Holy Spirit. An excellent read for both the people and Pastors, Christ lovers, and church leaders."

– David N. Wood P.A.O.C. Global Worker (Missionary)

Table of Contents

Introduction

Some spiritual concepts and practices which are in vogue in churches today are definitely ambiguous and often contradictory. When many of these concepts are evaluated, they are seen to lack a proper Biblical definition compared to clear Bible teaching.

Take, as an example, the term "church." Readers are liable to think that perhaps the building is being referenced, or perhaps the established organization is referenced. Admittedly, even those clerics whose responsibilities are the managing of the organization are under consideration.

Our efforts towards addressing any of these concepts and issues of the church are further compounded by the current, strong interest and support for these divergent concepts.

The history of the church in the western world is rife with the outcomes of the struggles that developed between the various stakeholders of the conflicting concepts of the church.

One author, Rodney Stark, in his book *One True God*, describes this conflict of interests and indicates it is because the church has had two conflicting identities.[1]

He identifies one group as *"the Church of Power,"* the ecclesiastical segment, and the other as *"the Church of Piety,"* the spiritual portion. He aptly shows how, over the four centuries following Constantine's foray into Christian issues, these two interests vied for supremacy and recognition. The large and vital question is: which of these interests truly represented what Christ had in mind when He stated, "I will build My church" (Matthew 16:18).

It will be the task of this work on the pages which follow to attempt to identify the true church that Christ spoke about and to understand its true character and mission today. The term "Church" will be largely set apart for clarity purposes. Because of this misunderstanding of titles, the term *"Community of the Spirit"* has been adopted as we investigate the relevancy of this term "church" for today's Christian edification. As the term "Church" is

---

[1] Rodney Stark, *One True God: Historical Consequences of Monotheism* (Princeton University Press, 1999)

used, Church will designate the organization. The term "church" will identify the organism which functions within the organization.

It is abundantly clear that references in the Bible which speak of the church always refer to the assembly or body of believers, not the organizational usurpation that gradually assumed the identity and prominence of control of the body. The Greek word *ekklesia,* often-translated *church,* refers to the "called out ones," the congregation.

You will no doubt recall from your own study that the Jewish religious regime that existed at Christ's time of ministry was always in conflict with Him and His message and His methodology. That existing religious system was not a true reflection or practice of the Mosaic Law but had become, over time, a legalistic, mean-faced, self-righteous hierarchical system devoid of grace, joy, or godliness.

The infusion of the Holy Spirit into the lives of the new believers after Pentecost brought a sharp rebuke to these leaders of that pharisaical religious system. However, we can also observe that these new believers energized by the Holy Spirit, in fact, demonstrated the true spirit of the Mosaic Law. This energized outbreak was a profound change in God's work among righteous, faithful men and women. This *Community of the Spirit* is also a sharp rebuke to the elite of today's religious practice. For example, this is evident in how the poor were cared for. Jesus was challenged on this point, (John 12:3–8):

³Then Mary took a pound of very costly oil of spikenard, anointed the feet of Jesus, and wiped His feet with her hair. And the house was filled with the fragrance of the oil.

⁴But one of His disciples, Judas Iscariot, Simon's *son,* who would betray Him, said,

⁵"Why was this fragrant oil not sold for three hundred denarii [about one year's wages for a worker] and given to the poor?"

⁶This he said, not that he cared for the poor, but because he was a thief, and had the moneybox; and he used to take what was put in it.

⁷But Jesus said, "Let her alone; she has kept this for the day of My burial.

⁸For the poor you have with you always, but Me you do not have always."

Jesus was quoting from Deuteronomy 15:11:

"For the poor will never cease from the land; therefore, I command you, saying, 'You shall open your hand wide to your brother, to your poor and your needy, in your land.'"

The case for Jesus' response shows that the care for the poor was to be extended well beyond the current practice; that was what Jesus was reminding them of when He was rebuked. Care for the poor is not intended to be an event, but a lifestyle.

~ PART ONE ~

The Mission Begins

The Day of Pentecost appears to be the birthday of the *Community of the Spirit*. This marvelous event was a manifestation of Christ's declaration to His followers, "Behold, I send the Promise of My Father upon you; but tarry in the city of Jerusalem until you are endued with power from on high" (Luke 24:49).

This event was also the point where the consequences of the new covenant, written in the blood of Christ, supersede the law and ordinances given to Moses in the Old Testament.

Galatians 3:24, 25:

[24]Therefore the law was our tutor *to bring us* to Christ, that we might be justified by faith. [25]But after faith has come, we are no longer under a tutor.

Luke 16:16:

The law and the prophets *were* until John. Since that time, the kingdom of God has been preached, and everyone is pressing into it.

Matthew 5:17:

"Do not think that I came to destroy the Law or the Prophets.

I did not come to destroy but to fulfill."

These scriptures and the outpouring of the Spirit sever the validity of the Old Testament ordinances and practices as a means of achieving merit or righteousness before God.

However, the door of opportunity puts the individual believer and the community, collectively, into a course of conduct where the practice of faith towards God is to become the spiritual form of exchange and interaction.

Perhaps we can extract from the Bible what the true mission and character of this *Community* is, so that we might move its origin and continual relevancy out from under the overburden of religious, cultural, and political dialogue. It often seems in a discussion of the true Church and its true identification, the *Community of the Spirit* is hampered by this institutionalized "church" dialogue. However, such a discussion is often deemed an attack on the Church. Our task is to clarify roles from a Biblical perspective, not to demean any sincere efforts which are advanced in order to serve Christ.

The genesis of the *Community of the Spirit*, of course, begins with the events which are recorded in the Bible following the Day of Pentecost. On this historic occasion, three thousand souls were added to the one hundred and twenty followers of Christ and were of those who had received the great outpouring of the Spirit, the fulfillment of the promise recorded in Joel 2:29: "And also on *My* menservants and on *My* maidservants I will pour out My Spirit in those days."

Acts 2:40, 41 records the reactions of this Pentecostal group:

[40]And with many other words he [Peter] testified and exhorted them, saying, "Be saved from this perverse generation."

[41]Then those who gladly received his word were baptized; and that day about three thousand souls were added *to them.*

[42]And they continued steadfastly in the apostles' doctrine and fellowship, in the breaking of bread, and in prayers.

This is also the fruit of John's prophecy of Matthew 3:11: "He [Jesus] will baptize you with the Holy Spirit and fire."

Struggle for Emancipation

We must understand that those new converts to Christ did not join an ongoing established religious organization, nor was this a formation of a new sect of the Jewish religion as some thought then.

This historical recorded event was a new and radical departure, both culturally and spiritually. This momentous event immediately included all common men and women and would eventually embrace the despised Gentiles. This event severed forever the efficacy of the Old Testament sacrifices and rituals before a righteous God. The Old Testament practices became null and void as Christ demonstrated by His death and resurrection that the old covenant had been completed and fulfilled (Matthew 5:17). A new practice of personal faith overtook the law of works. The centerpiece of religious sacrifice was soon ended by the destruction of the temple in 70 A.D. Since then, no legitimate place of sacrifice has been established because He, Jesus, became the ultimate and final sacrifice.

The Old Testament covenant and religious regime was changed forever by the New Covenant established by Jesus's sacrifice. The status of the common men and women of faith was considered by Pharisees to be insignificant under the prevailing religious legalism and segregation under the Old Covenant. They now were chosen and empowered by the Lord to become functionaries or witnesses of resurrection power. At that point in history, it was an unheard-of action to give everyday people an important status and function without having a legally appointed or inherited office.

Martin Luther coined the phrase, "*the Priesthood of Believers*," after the scripture, "and has made us kings and priests to His God and Father" (Revelation 1:6). This appointment by Christ can only exist in *the Church of Piety* and not at all in *the Church of Power*.

Martin Luther (1483–1546), in his time and in his spiritual struggle to find acceptance with God, provides us with a suitable starting point which will address our topic. He, like many today, struggled with a repressive, unrelenting regime of religious duties and exercises imposed first by the pharisaical systems, then by the Roman Church. Peace with God was like a shadow on a distant horizon. Finally, the scriptures, illuminated by the Holy Spirit, opened Luther's heart and understanding. His release from this oppressive religious regime came as he read Romans 1:16, 17:

[16]For I am not ashamed of the gospel of Christ, for it is the power of God to salvation for everyone who believes, for the Jew first and also for the Greek.

[17]For in it, the righteousness of God is revealed from faith to faith; as it is written, "*The just shall live by faith.*"

Just as easily, Luther saw that all his doubts about his own unrighteousness and his ineffective religious acts were woefully inadequate in his search to find a place of favor with God. It became clear to him that faith in Christ was the sum total of all that God required of him to secure his relationship with God. A vigorous religious life encumbered with all forms of duties, strife, and self-doubt fell away as he saw the truth of God's plan for mankind's redemption for the first time.

The real remedy for a shattered emotional life and the sense of our inadequacy before God is found in receiving into our hearts the truth about God's promises and His redemptive provisions which are only to be found in Christ.

God's light will always assuage the works of darkness and confusion. As Psalm 119:105 states: "Your word is a lamp to my feet and a light to my path."

Of such are the true disciples of Christ in the *Community of the Spirit*, people who have found a personal, not a collective, faith in Christ.

Imagine, if you will, what emotional and soul-searching struggles new believers encounter as they come to faith in Christ. New concepts which conflict with past experiences arise. Experiences on which they have built their approach to life are now part of a new struggle. They will even experience a new sense of self-awareness as "all things become new" (2 Corinthians 5:17). No institutionally developed and imposed system can provide the "new" relationship with Christ.

Coming to faith in Christ presents many truths which are "positional"; that is, that these truths or values have been achieved for us by Christ's death and resurrection. They have been presented to God on our behalf and can never be accomplished in any concrete form by our striving in our religious endeavors.

Our "positions" are observed by a Holy God as He has accepted Christ's works on our behalf.

Sanctification is a reality, holiness is a reality, but the reality is expressed in our lives as we daily follow Christ and His direction for our lives. These attributes and other spiritual values are never fully achievable in the flesh but a present reality in the Spirit because of God's considerable work redemption.

Loving a Loving God

The concept of the "Fatherhood of God" must raise a confusing specter for someone who has experienced the trauma of a troubled childhood. Experiences arising from growing up with abusive, overbearing, and uncaring fathers, for instance, irritate regressed feelings. These emotional scars incurred then must now compete with the concept of an ever-loving Heavenly Father. These traumatic childhood experiences can often imprint a sense which is not easily dismissed. Simply hearing a selection of scriptures which describe the Heavenly Father's love for them does not easily heal these memories.

Or perhaps a new believer may have grown up under the regime of always having to please an earthly father as a precondition to them receiving some sought-after favor or expression of love. For some seekers, these experiences may have had wicked or unpleasant negative outcomes. These unhappy circumstances from our past negatively impress and suppress the spirit of people and their faith processes when it comes to grappling with their understanding of the favor of a "Heavenly Father."

So easily this traumatized, negative mindset finds itself falling into a religious legalistic trap. What was intended, by Christ's death and resurrection, to provide unconditional promises and provisions are soon seen to require some demonstrable religious action in order to be considered acceptable to God. From this poorly constructed thought process, a legalistic works regime fully follows. If "faith without works is dead" (James 2:26); then works without faith is doubly so.

Under misguided leadership, many of these victims are defrauded of their true Christian heritage. Many may never come to experience the true nature of God's love for them. This condition of legalistic struggles will hinder these victims from "growing in grace and the knowledge of God" (2 Peter 3:18). They soon fall victim, also, to the accusations of inadequacy by the devil and are forever treading on a probationary turnstile.

Matthew 6:28: "Consider the lilies of the field, how they grow: they neither toil nor spin," Jesus said to His seekers.

John, the beloved disciple of Christ, puts forward some great ideas which will define our subject of acceptability before God. These concepts are recorded for our instruction and edification in the Book of 1 John.

On the subject of our status before a loving God, John states, "Beloved, now we are children of God" (I John 3:2). John, herein, establishes our privileged position and status before a loving God; that is, that we presently, today, have a right of heritage and authorization before Him. The scope and character of this position is not based on our own qualities of character or achievement, but on Christ's character and "*sinlessness*" and His sacrificial and propitious death on the cross (I John 2:2; Romans 3:25).

It's Not About You

In a time in society when we are forever inundated with a *me-centered* culture, there is a dangerous swampland to be avoided in understanding our relationship with God.

Recently, a former professional football star commenting on his own coming to faith stated, "I guess that God just needed another fullback on his team." We need to keep the ground clear on this subject. God does not need football stars on his team and neither does He save football stars for His team. He saves sinners! Any other interjection of values or worthiness simply demeans Christ's propitious payment for our souls (1 John 4:9–10).

Augustine said, "For grace is not given because we have done good works, but in order that we may be able to do them."

God loves mankind, all of us. Why? And why you and me in particular? Because this love extended through salvation is true to His nature and character. God is love! It may deflate some of our self-esteem to know that we have brought nothing of personal worth to God's call to salvation. We have nothing to offer in exchange for His love. Only faith will suffice, and that faith is a gift from God.

Martin Luther said, "I am not loved because I am valuable, I am valuable because I am loved."

We may feel humbled by that thought; however, by it we gain a profound freedom from the accuser of the brethren, the devil, when we grasp this concept.

The devil offers his barbs; he says, "you are not worthy." Rather than trying to justify ourselves, we can acknowledge our unworthiness and direct the devil to address Jesus on the subject. Jesus Christ is our constant Advocate before the throne of grace (I John 2:1; Hebrews 7:25).

We are also freed from brotherly envy and strife as we walk out our salvation daily. As sinners, all saved by grace, we have no rank or rating before Christ as he presents us before the throne of God.

We cannot truly complete, with any degree of accuracy and honesty, the challenging sentence:

"God loves me because I... (*insert your own words*)..."

The statement, "I am not loved because I am valuable, but I am valuable because I am loved," begins to open our understanding to God's love for us which was provided for our redemption and blessing.

The way forward is very poignantly demonstrated by 1 John 4:10: "In this is love, not that we loved God, but that He loved us and sent His Son *to be* the propitiation [appeasement] for our sins." Do you begin to see that the truth begins to walk us away from our own efforts and to show us His provisions that are accessed by faith?

The riddle of God's love is soon taken away from liturgy and dogma and is placed squarely on our personal faith in Christ's shed blood for all of us, unworthy though we are. Ascribed church liturgy, dogma, and ritual or penance of various sorts, will not begin to open the doors of His love. Any other method or means, but the love and blood of Jesus begins to evoke the truth (of John 10:1) that speaks of a thief who chooses to approach God by any other means or method.

"Most assuredly, I say to you, he who does not enter the sheepfold by the door, but climbs up some other way, the same is a thief and a robber" (John 10:1).

A Relevant Church

When we state that the agreement of our spirit with God does not begin with ourselves, we are not showing support for the Calvinist doctrine of election before God. Instead, we are demonstrating that our pathway to God is one of His provision and choice, "For by grace have you been saved through faith, and that not of yourselves; it is a gift from God" (Ephesians 2.8). But the scripture plainly shows that we are admonished to exercise our faith towards His provision, "That if you confess with your mouth the Lord Jesus and believe in your heart that God has raised Him from the dead, you will be saved" (Romans 10:9). The scripture plainly shows we are admonished to exercise our faith towards His provision.

We can easily observe that the lost world, by and large, has sidelined the relevance of the modern church as an archaic institution. This attitude denies the facts that our present secular cultures have produced enormous problems which have diminished the value and purpose of life. Humanism of various stripes has been tried and found wanting.

The great and profound social and moral achievements since Christ came into history, however, need to be seen as the outcome of Christian teaching and practice wherever and whenever it occurred. Just compare the issue of human rights and charity in countries that have no Christian heritage. Take slavery as an example.

The theological conclusion that slavery is sinful has been unique to Christianity. A second factor is that of the major world faiths; only Christianity has devoted serious and sustained attention to human rights as opposed to human duties. Put another way, the other great faiths minimize individualism and stress collective obligations.

Rodney Stark [2]

This denial of Christian values by the world is, of course, a deviant result of the increased superstition that secular, materialistic humanism would provide as a means of upward mobility of the human spirit. The western Christian world, pioneering breakthroughs in every discipline of learning and enlightenment of the soul, holds a great debt to the fearless suffering of men of faith over the centuries who preached the freedom of faith.

The Church has become intimidated by many such worldly attitudes and values which plot against the fundamental teaching which Christ gave to the early church. The church has retreated from the mandate to *"go into the world and preach the word"* and to be *salt and light*. Instead of taking the baton of the ages, it has become, to too great a measure, an empty shell bent on becoming ingrown and self-serving. What we seem to be pressing our energies into, it could be said, is trying display of confidence. This confidence arises as we continually refresh our understanding that we are serving a more noble cause and a calling from the eternal God who sent His only Son into the world to redeem us.

---

[2] Rodney Stark, *THE VICTORY OF REASON* (Random House Trade Paperbacks Edition, New York, NY 10022, ©2005) 30,31

God's love is equally offered to all who come to Him in faith. We must .ever lose touch with the point of our own equality before God as we develop and otherwise grow our relationship.

We are also freed from a sense of *measuring up* by the knowledge that this love agreement is based on Christ's character and not ours.

The referenced verse of scripture, "In this is love, not that we loved God, but that He loved us," (I John 4:10) demonstrates that this compact of love begins justifiably with God. God took this first initiative to redeem us. This action taken by God is without prior conditions on our part. This action allows and even persuades us to respond with our own expressions of love towards Him and also to love all whom He has called in such fashion.

When we begin to appreciate the cost of our redemption, the sacrificial death of Christ to redeem us from our sin and its eternal penalty, we begin to responsively return this love.

"In this is love, not that we loved God, but that He loved us and sent His Son to be the propitiation for our sins" (1 John 4:10).

Our response, if we understand the enormous cost rightly, should be untainted with religiosity or any sense of our own personal worth.

Admittedly, it may be difficult for some people of a religious bent to accept their own personal nothingness before a loving God; however, our sense of worthlessness before God is where the heart of our freedom from selfish interest is to be found.

This is also the humble beginning of a fruitful walk of faith with Him.

Forever we must be found to not be postulating or promoting our worth as a part of our redemption and our inheritance of the promises and blessings of God.

There is an acid test of our understanding and acceptance of the fact that God is the initiator of the profound love relationship. We can read this fact portrayed in I John 4:18; "There is no fear in love; but perfect love casts out fear, because fear involves torment. But he who fears has not been made perfect in love." Overt fear on our part is a demonstration of our lack of understanding His perfect love.

It is evident that many believers who struggle with their acceptability before God, especially in times of doubt and trial common to us all, have not been made perfect in love. We desperately need to examine the content of our faith and why our understanding of God's abiding and effective love for us is being blocked. Perhaps the blockage is caused by our self-imposed religious conditioning.

He loved us, that is the primary principle of our love relationship. It is at this point that we are made free of fear, uncertainty, and confusion, and we begin a response of love towards Him. We abandon our self-interest as we submit ourselves to His eternal love. God is love. We need not ever think that He is about to terrorize our faith; God doesn't ever do this to His own.

The predictable return of confidence towards God and our role of faith in this world allows us to get on with our calling to love one another. Our faith is unshackled as we are perfected in this profound love compact.

Remember that Christ gave us only two commandments to fulfill in the New Testament. The first was to love God, and the second was to love others as ourselves (Matthew 22:37–40). In doing so, we also complete the requirements of the Spirit of the Old Testament law. God loved us so profoundly that He sent His only Son to be the propitiation for our sins (I John 2:2). Understanding this truth causes a profound *letting go*, a release of uncertain fears; fears that constrict our faith and that plague our confidence towards God.

A New Direction for the Community

There is an immense calmness and lack of external constraint to be found within the *Community of the Spirit* as love and mercy take hold. Whether in revival or in historical practice, Christian mercy and its partner love find fruit in peaceful relationships. Consider this excerpt from Tertullian, a revered church father (155–222 AD), in his work *Apology* wrote:

"There is no buying and selling of any sort of things of God. Though we have our treasure chest, it is not made up of purchase money, as of a religion that has its price. On the monthly day, if he likes, each puts in a small donation, but only if it be his pleasure, and only if he is able, for there is no compulsion; all is voluntary. These gifts are, as it were, piety's deposit funds. For they are not taken thence and spent on feasts and drinking bouts and eating houses (the normal pagan practice), but to supply the wants of boys and girls destitute of means and parents, and of old persons confined now to houses; such too as have suffered shipwreck; and if there happen to be any in the mines, or banished to the islands, or shut up in prisons, for nothing but their fidelity to the cause of God's church, they become nurslings of their confession."

You may readily see that this testimony offered by the early church following Jesus's resurrection was not something which was acted upon out of obligation or dogma. The Spirit which empowered this body of believers of the *Community of the Spirit* was still very much at work. This love relationship had not yet been corrupted with liturgy, dogma, or ecclesiastical control.

These charitable activities were possible because only Christianity generated a true community of believers, just as we have observed from Acts 2, not just clients as the pagan religions produced.

It is worth noting that after the Church was given the nod of approval by Constantine, successive Caesars tried to stimulate the various pagan groups to demonstrate charity as a means of convincing the Roman population to return to paganism. This Caesarian venture was a failure mainly because paganism and, for that matter, various sects and cults are self-seeking and do not experience the release which knowing the love of God provides.

These pagan ventures spent their efforts trying to appease their angry and uncaring gods, so-called. Self-interest was their driving force. We, however, have experienced how God loves us; ever, always.

Lavish Beginnings

Nearly twenty centuries have passed on into history since that day when God shook up the world's self-serving religious systems. This Day of Pentecost forever altered the course of world religion; altered in that its revitalized scope included all the known world and the world yet to be discovered. God no longer dealt exclusively with His chosen people, the Jews; as the fulfillment of Joel's prophecy of a pouring out of God's own Holy Spirit upon "all flesh" brought the Gentile world under His plan for the future (Acts 2:16–21), (Joel 2:28–32):

[16]But this is what was spoken by the prophet Joel:
[17]And it shall come to pass in the last days, says God,
That I will pour out of My Spirit on all flesh;
Your sons and your daughters shall prophecy,
Your young men shall see visions,
Your old men shall dream dreams.
[18]And on My menservants and on My maidservants
I will pour out My Spirit in those days;
And they shall prophecy.
[19]I will show wonders in heaven above
And signs in the earth beneath:
Blood and fire and vapor of smoke.
[20]The sun shall be turned into darkness,
And the moon into blood,

Before the coming of the great and awesome day of the LORD.
²¹And it shall come to pass
That whoever calls on the name of the LORD
Shall be saved.

It will benefit our study to read of how this was worked out in the Gentile world. The account is found in Acts chapters 10:1 through 11:18; below is a short portion of the script:

¹⁴But Peter said, "Not so, Lord! For I have never eaten anything common or unclean."

¹⁵And a voice *spoke* to him again the second time, "What God has cleansed you must not call common."

¹⁶This was done three times. And the object was taken up into heaven again.

¹⁷Now while Peter wondered within himself what this vision which he had seen meant, behold, the men who had been sent from Cornelius had made inquiry for Simon's house, and stood before the gate.

¹⁸And they called and asked whether Simon, whose surname was Peter, was lodging there.

We also read how Peter responded to critics of his visit to the home of Cornelius, the Gentile centurion of the city of Caesarea (Acts 15:8, 9):

⁸So God, who knows the heart, acknowledged them by giving them the Holy Spirit, just as *He did* to us,

⁹and made no distinction between us and them, purifying their hearts by faith.

Some secular historians, lately, have called his newly devised *Community of the Spirit* merely an extension of the Jewish religion, a Jewish sect if you will. But because the *all flesh* component of this new sovereign move brought the Gentiles under His full blessing (above), its Jewishness, of tradition and ritual, was very soon eclipsed by an original demonstration of spiritual participation by the Gentile masses as well. The ritualistic character was soon to be replaced with energetic worship and preaching and practices of faith.

The new Christian behavior was a radical departure from a long Hebrew tradition which had followed Moses's Law for thousands of years. This new action of faith transformed it into the kingdom of God. Moses, you will recall, brought approximately 2 million slaves, who had served Egyptian masters for 400 years, out of bondage (Book of Exodus). These Hebrew slaves would have retained no culture of their own or religious form of their own to depend on in their newfound place in history. Remember that this was before God gave Moses the Ten Commandments. We need to realize that Moses was not called to start a new national religion. What he was told by God to give the Hebrews was a new constitution and laws. These commandments were to mold them into a righteous and holy nation unto God Himself (Exodus 19:6, 7). Jewish law soon became ritualized and formalized so rigidly that it fought against the very freedom of faith which was intended and which Jesus taught in His days of ministry.

As well, Jesus did not come to start a new religion but to establish the kingdom of God. Our New Testament including Christ's teachings were provided as the statutes and instructions to show us, today, how this kingdom of God should function and conduct itself. It, too, quickly became rigid and dogmatic. Whereas Jesus established a spiritual kingdom, men soon strived to establish it as a worldly kingdom.

Rome and many other religious ventures soon fell into kingdom building with their own agendas for how this should play out into society. Jesus, however, said He would build His church.

There's a Direct Link Between Our Spirit and Our Spunk

First century Christians were profoundly outlooking in their efforts to redeem the lost by the spread of the gospel instead of establishing doctrinal practices of self-defense. They were aggressive in their practices and expectation, no doubt partly because of the idea of the soon return of Jesus to set up His own kingdom of heaven.

The regressive mindset which followed Constantine's captivity of the *Community of the Spirit* was no doubt partially fueled by the need to build, on earth, the kingdom which Christ said He would build himself.

This unseen kingdom is still very successfully being built throughout the world and indeed throughout history as multitudes of hearts are converted to His kingdom. And this despite the very same dangers and opposition that the early church faced.

Many latter-day advocates of resurrecting the tenets of the Law as an expanded means of credibility try to impose some of that Old Testament religious form as a means of establishing some new level of righteousness.

Jesus declared, "The law and the prophets *were* until John. Since that time, the kingdom of God has been preached, and everyone is pressing into it" (Luke 16:16). Romans 10:4 states, "For Christ is the end of the law for righteousness to everyone who believes." The old covenant of works and sacrifices has been forever replaced by a covenant of faith in the finished work of Christ on Calvary. What could be clearer than that?

Although this new kingdom of God carried with it shades and shadows of the fulfilled law, this kingdom's message soon showed us the inadequacy of the Law's capacity to provide righteousness. The kingdom of God's message, since then, has been preached and established, and the *Community of the Spirit* has ventured on. Venture on it did, despite persecution and fraudulent behavior on the part of some of its adherents and masters, so called.

The world that the apostles ventured into with the new message of faith was mostly a world of some form of unfriendly paganism; that is, except for the Jewish faith which was quite widespread over the Roman Empire; but it did not take kindly either to the conversion of its population.

So this new faith in Christ began to march into a prejudicial atmosphere; firstly, with one hundred and twenty recipients of the Holy Spirit, and then immediately by the addition of three thousand on the day of this outpouring (Acts 2:41). Historically, conversion of Jews on this scale was not taken as a light event. Despite persecution, torture, and death, it became the strident element of change which eroded the might of the pagan Roman Empire.

The features of the church established in Acts 2 quite simply changed the heart of the Roman Empire by converting Roman society to Christianity. It is well documented by historians that nearly fifty percent of the Roman Empire had become Christian by 400 AD, a momentous achievement of change by any standard.

This Church Age began almost in an instant on the famous Day of Pentecost by a regenerative and empowering work of the Holy Spirit in men's hearts.

A review of the Gospels reveals the religious posture of Jesus's day. It was overtly bigoted, radical, and mean-spirited. Religious leaders were ready, at any presumed action of non-compliance, to kill any detractors by lawful or other means. These same religious leaders had disenfranchised the very people who Christ met with and ministered to. These leaders considered the poor and sinful people to be outside the pale of a holy and severe God's interest.

Suddenly at Pentecost, the energy of the Holy Spirit changed the hearts and motivation of people of faith. Suddenly, the unloved and neglected became the focus of changed people's hearts as they went about providing care for any in need among the disenfranchised.

The obvious question to be asked is; what was at the heart of this new religion that so affected the pagan masses? What was this new covenant all about?

Wherever in the world this new "church" has emerged, it has been of a different energy and character than the Mosaic institutions were able to manifest. The Law, given to the Hebrew slaves after their exodus from Egypt, helped them change from their bondage mentality as they lived alongside an Egyptian pagan society. The Law transformed them into a unique nation among pagans (Deuteronomy 4:1–8). The Bible informs that they prospered under God's hand as long as they obeyed this law.

Filling the Whole Earth

Unlike any other religious movement before the coming of Christ or since His death and resurrection, the Christian message has gone out to "fill the whole earth" (Matthew 24:14). First, it is credited, by many reputable scholars, with weakening the oppressive pagan strength of Rome and becoming the spiritual strength of the pre-papal Christians who continued to be salt and light wherever they went.

[13]"You are the salt of the earth; but if the salt loses its flavor, how shall it be seasoned? It is then good for nothing but to be thrown out and trampled underfoot by men.

[14]"You are the light of the world. A city that is set on a hill cannot be hidden (Matthew 5:13, 14).

[5]…the word of the truth, the gospel

[6]that has come to you. All over the world this gospel is bearing fruit and growing, just as it has been doing among you since the day you heard and understood God's grace in all its truth (Colossians 1:5,6 NIV).

This phenomenal growth of the infant church has continued to fill the whole earth just as Daniel prophesied; "And the stone that struck the image became a great mountain and filled the whole earth" (Daniel 2:35b). There is hardly a corner of the earth where the gospel has not had an effect on culture and sin's reign.

This action was prophesied by the prophet Daniel about four hundred years earlier; this amazing story is found in the Book of Daniel, chapter two. The Great King of Babylon, Nebuchadnezzar, had a dream and was so troubled that he could not sleep (verse 1). He called for "the magicians, astrologers, sorcerers, and the Chaldeans to tell him his dreams" (verse 2). When they could not, "he was angry and very furious and gave the command to destroy all the wise *men* of Babylon. So the decree went out, and they began killing the wise *men*; and they sought Daniel and his companions, to kill them" (verses 12, 13). In due time, after he and his companions had sought "mercies from the God of heaven concerning this secret" (verse 18), it came about that "the secret was revealed to Daniel in a night vision" (verse 19).

He was able to tell the king his dream and also the interpretation:

³¹"You, O king, were watching, and behold, a great image! This great image, whose splendor *was* excellent, stood before you, and its form *was* awesome.

³²This image's head was of fine gold, its chest and arms of silver, its belly and thighs of bronze

³³its legs of iron, its feet partly of iron and partly of clay

³⁴You watched while a stone was cut without hands, which truck the image on its feet of iron and clay and broke them in pieces.

³⁵Then the iron, the clay, the bronze, the silver, and the gold were crushed together, and became like chaff from the summer threshing floors; the wind carried them away so that no trace of them was found. And the stone that struck the image became a great mountain and filled the whole earth.

³⁶This is the dream. Now we will tell the interpretation of it before the king.

⁴⁰And the fourth kingdom shall be as strong as iron, inasmuch as iron breaks in pieces and shatters everything" (Daniel 2:31–40).

It has been agreed by many Biblical scholars that the great image of Daniel's vision identified the Roman Empire as the "legs of iron" (vs. 33). The stone mentioned here, "cut out without hands" (vs. 34) is Jesus and the kingdom which He introduced.

⁴⁴"…the God of heaven will set up a kingdom which shall never be destroyed; and the kingdom shall not be left to other people; it shall break in pieces and consume all these kingdoms, and it shall stand forever.

⁴⁵Inasmuch as you saw that the stone was cut out of the mountain without hands, and that it broke in pieces the iron, the bronze, the clay, the silver, and the gold—the great God has made known to the king what will come to pass after this. The dream is certain, and its interpretation is sure" (Daniel 2:44, 45).

Jesus's life and ministry echoed the message of this prophecy; "And this gospel of the kingdom will be preached in all the world as a witness to all the nations, and then the end will come" (Matthew 24:14).

Form and Substance

Throughout the centuries since Christ came to die for our freedom from the penalty of sin and rebellion, and since that awesome day when the Spirit of God was poured out on those men and women of faith, people have struggled with finding the correct forms of expression of the effects of their personal redemption and worshipful living.

History has shown us that the Church made efforts to understand and to grasp this freedom of faith. Villains and dictators of a religious bent have tried to capture the energy expressed by a redeemed body of people in order to serve their own agendas and ambitions. That has always been the case. So it was with Simon the sorcerer's goal (Acts 8:18). From this we have Simony, greedy gain in the so-called "service of the Lord."

The church, which was born full of energy and given a mandate from the Lord to "go into all the world and preach the gospel" (Mark 16:15), grappled for form and substance but mainly used everyday expressions of friendship, caring, and sharing as their methodology in carrying the gospel message.

Unlike any other religious movement before or since, the Christian message has gone out to fill the whole earth, (Daniel 2:35).

Since the first days of the Spirit of God awakening faith in God and the display of the fruit of the Spirit and this power of God, it has been a dedicated work of evil men to hijack this energy of the Spirit in men. Jesus said, "Even you [scribes and Pharisees] outwardly appear righteous to men, but inside you are full of hypocrisy and lawlessness" (Matthew 23:28).

So it has been ever since that day. Men, acting as opportunists, have set about to control, manage, or otherwise take ownership of God's kingdom and to use the *Community of the Spirit* to exercise political and spiritual power.

Several authors have shown how the Church of Rome quickly attracted unscrupulous men to take up positions of authority in the church. Rodney Stark in his books on Christian beginnings states that: "the funding of the Christian faith by Rome as the State Church precipitated a stampede of the sons of the nobility into the Church offices."[3] Because the church was well funded by the state, it attracted all manner of unscrupulous men, and there began the mixing of the water into the wine. The initial message was quickly diluted by political ambition.

Prior to Constantine's nod, it was illegal for Christians to own Church property. Church offices, after this state approval, were assumed by advantage or outright purchase. This is the point at which the Church began the aggrandizement of buildings which were built in the Roman pagan manner. This so-called "place of worship" copied the Basilica, which had become the throne room and an assembly place for the elite; not a place that was friendly to the poor masses.

The Church of Power brought with it the Roman practice of assimilating or encapsulating the pagan religions of its conquered peoples. Not only were the foreign gods received into the alloy of religion, but the Church of Rome soon also adopted the pagan idols, symbolism, and feast days along with the

---

[3] Rodney Stark, The Triumph of Christianity (Harper Collins, 2011), 299

empire's practices of governance and hierarchical regimes. The Greek poet Hesiod claimed there were 30,000 distinct gods.[4]

Whenever the Church ventures led them to conquer new areas and populations, it was not a work of missionizing the masses as the apostles had done, but the religious subjugation and baptizing of leaders.

In subduing these areas, they, the Roman church, also assimilated much of these pagan religions. Long dead pagan heroes and *saints* were *baptized* into the Roman faith along with their festivals, celebrations, and holy days.

God Reforms Idolatry

Godly men of the Reformation tried to strip away much of these pagan influences from their newfound faith in the authority of the Bible but did not completely succeed. Church government structures and liturgies still retained some deviant practices as well as corrupted doctrines adopted with their new church authority. Some of these divisive issues plague the purity of Christianity today. Some of these divisive issues are what define many of our doctrinal camps as we try to serve the Lord with a pure conscience.

An example of the early church fathers, who were previously schooled in Greek philosophy erred in that, after coming to faith in Christ, taught that this new Christian religion was to be understood by viewing it through the Greek humanistic and philosophical mindset. This issue, "Christian humanism," is still with us today. We desperately need to get back to basics if the church is to continue to have a witness worthy of Christ.

In a study of the infant body of believers we find in Acts 2, it appears that a miracle has taken place in preserving the essence of the Day of Pentecost. The church's original call has not been diminished despite Roman opposition, persecution, usurping of governance, and changes by imposition of the church's intended purpose of being "salt and light" (Matthew 5:13–16).

Strife, debate, war, and heresy as well have not obliterated the original purpose of the Lord.

It seems that whenever an overloading threat to the church (true believers) was raised up, God sovereignly made a side step from under the overburden of hypocrisy and idolatry, and the church *rolled on.*

By the time of John Knox (1513–1572), the Scottish reformer, an oppressive Roman religion had taken hold and almost smothered the true faith of the apostles. John Knox met this error head on and succeeded in shutting down its oppressive advantage. The "just shall live by faith" premise (Romans

---

[4] Rodney Stark, Cities of God, (Grant, 1986), 45

1:17 & Habakkuk 2:4) of other reformers like: Luther (1483–1546), German; Calvin (1509–1564), French; as well as Zwingli (1484–1531), Swiss; won the day. It is recorded of John Knox's ministry that Queen Mary and the bishops cringed in fear when John Knox prayed. The opposition of the Reformers left Rome largely holding an empty religious bag as their prize, and the Church rolled on.

In England, the Anglican Church that King Henry the VIII (1494–1547) assumed leadership of became so oppressive and intolerant of the non-conformers that they were pursued by the law of the land. You will recall the life of John Bunyan (1628–1688), English writer (The Pilgrim's Progress) and Baptist preacher, who tried to preach the softer side of the gospel of grace and who was jailed for his efforts.

These English non-conformers soon applied for, and received, a charter of the king to establish colonies in the Americas. From this original charter came the edict, "One nation under God," and the United States of America began to flourish under the free sound of the gospel. So God has repeatedly side stepped the oppression of evil men which was used to suppress the gospel.

When the aforementioned *Church of Power* ascended to control, the monastic movement, with a sincere devotion to Christ, was born. It was essentially a protest movement which tried to escape the evils of Rome. It soon moved out from under the oppression, corruption, and restriction of Rome. As men of honest motivation read the Bible as it was made available, they experienced life-changing issues of faith. These men taught and acted out new practices of charity and help, much as the men and women of Acts 2. But again, who can count the endless persecution and martyrdom these people experienced as they rose to a new spiritual maturity.

The Celtic Church of Ireland began soon after Rome's corruption took hold. A profound work of teaching and charity lifted the people of Ireland out of their poverty and misery. Schools were established and improvements to husbandry helped to change this primitive society. The Celtic Church monks performed worthy works until their ministry was "assumed" by Roman authority prior to the change of the first millennium (1000 AD).

Russia, China, and other oppressive powers sought to extinguish the church's faith in their time by political and military means, but the church grew even more under these vile means. Historically, it seems that the church under stress is capable of shining its light into dark places. The contrast of light and darkness makes the gospel of the kingdom more attractive than the negative persuasiveness of persecutions.

When the communist government in China evicted the foreign missionaries in 1948, detractors of Christianity's resilience scornfully stated that these "rice Christians" would soon disappear. They wrongfully taught that the Chinese believers were not sincere, but attended and were compliant because rice was provided by the missionaries. Instead of disappearing, the underground church grew to what is thought to be one hundred million as a conservative count today. The church in China and Russia and all opposing countries continues to grow even today under extreme conditions.

As Jesus said, "I will build My church and the gates of hell will not prevail against it" (Matthew 16:18).

Even Abraham looked forward to "the city of God whose builder and maker is God" (Hebrews 11:10).

The study of church history is amazing for, no doubt, it is a study of a miracle which is still in play. We are the inheritors of Jesus's prophecy, "And this gospel of the kingdom will be preached in all the world as a witness to all the nations, and then the end will come" (Matthew 24:14).

Questions About the Early Church

A study of this early church model has left me with at least four basic questions about its energy and vitality. This work will attempt to answer these questions that have been raised. These basic questions are:

1. What is the true nature, which was and continues to be found, working through the body of believers?
2. How can this energy be liberated from the damaging control of self-seeking interests?
3. What does this church look like and act like when it is functioning as a *Community of the Spirit*?
4. How can this energy be developed and directed, and then put into everyday practice today in a vital way?

Sincere efforts directed towards restoring the original Day of Pentecost model of the infant church to its original power and purity sometimes fall into the same pitfalls, hurdles, and errors of the past. We seem to be able to develop practices, rules, and governance, but somehow our actions miss the spiritual energy needed to move the church forwards. Somehow, we just end up serving the rules and practices, "the letter of the law," but not the spirit of the freedom of faith.

An advocacy directed towards using the local house church as the best overall model does not take into consideration that there has been a massive population growth since the first century. A house church model will never serve a city population of over a million people. Even having many house churches in a large city would mean that the coordination and unification of such a venture would create a loss of community. Centralization or structure of authority and decision making in remote locations by men who were untouched by local issues would then be the result.

The Roman model of management produced an authoritarian regime which created a top-down system which mostly conflicted with and overrode the legitimacy of the revelation of Jesus and the prompting of the Holy Spirit to individuals.

The church, you may recall, was founded on response to the message of personal faith in Jesus. "You must be born again," Jesus declared to Nicodemus, the ruler of the Jews (John 3:3).

Over the centuries since Christ shed His blood for our many sins, several divergent structures and doctrines of organized Christianity have been tried. These were touted as the best models based on extra-Biblical information. It seems that "progressive" leaders think that if you create a *best model*, then blessing and success will follow.

The main problem with the top-down model of authority and control is that, by default, the upper levels must do the heavy lifting. They also protect their vested interest in their own structures and programs. The lower echelons are disenfranchised by this stance and they do little of the necessary work of reaching the lost and serving the needs of the destitute. The energy of the body of believers is nullified and dismissed as destructive to regime order. In its place, only obedience to the top levels is appreciated. State churches work in collusion with the state to provide a compliant population in support of the state and the restrictions, a condition imposed for state sponsorship.

Since the Day of Pentecost's blessing or the fulfillment of the Promise of God (Acts 2:33), its effects were soon spread well beyond the borders of Israel. The Gentile world was as foreign to this gospel as the newly liberated Hebrew slaves were to Moses's Law.

Features of the Community of the Spirit

If we study this outbreak of God's Spirit and its immediate result on the Day of Pentecost, we can easily extract what the character of the infant church was. We can also see what it was not about as this infant entity began to find its feet and mission.

(Please read carefully our central scripture reference. Try to find yourself in this scenario.)

A Vital Church Grows
ACTS 2:40–47, (NKJV)

[40]And with many other words he [Peter] testified and exhorted them, saying, "Be saved from this perverse generation."

[41]Then those who gladly received his word were baptized; and that day about three thousand souls were added *to them*.

[42]And they continued steadfastly in the apostles' doctrine and fellowship, in the breaking of bread, and in prayers.

[43]Then fear came upon every soul, and many wonders and signs were done through the apostles.

[44]Now all who believed were together, and had all things in common,

[45]and sold their possessions and goods, and divided them among all, as anyone had need.

[46]So continuing daily with one accord in the temple, and breaking bread from house to house, they ate their food with gladness and simplicity of heart,

[47]praising God and having favor with all the people. And the Lord added to the church daily those who were being saved.

This scripture plainly shows us the *Community of the Spirit* in its infancy.

It doesn't appear that any church council was called to flesh out a new religious venture or to determine its structure or guidelines for operation. These Holy Spirit infused men and women acted upon the deficient issues of their society and were motivated by a charitable turn of heart.

It is encouraging to see that though this new body of believers were seen as reactive, they, in fact, were also fulfilling the spiritual requirements of the Mosaic Law. Their charitable acts did not conflict with the Law, but they did rile the religious leaders, as they found that these acts of charity surpassed the restrictions of their religious tradition. A religious tradition is always subject to contradiction in light of the work of the Spirit of God.

As we progress in our study, we will highlight fifteen features of this New Testament Church which made their actions so dynamic and effective in upsetting the evil of the pagan world and the Jewish culture of the day:

1. Enthusiasm
2. Baptism
3. Coming Together
4. Teaching
5. Fellowship
6. Sharing of Food
7. Sharing of Possessions
8. Agreement (Concord)
9. Gladness and Simplicity
10. Praising God
11. Kindness to Those Around
12. Receiving New Members
13. Sharing the Gospel
14. Signs and Wonders
15. Prayer

You can find a descriptive list of these features beginning at page 45.

Christ founded neither a church nor a state; He handed over no laws, nor government, nor any form of external authority; but He tried to write the law of God in the hearts of men in order that they might govern themselves.

Hubert Newton (1830–1896)

What seems to be a very plain and straightforward statement offered from an American astronomer and mathematician is not so uncomplicated after all. It is, however, a profound statement which provokes the question, where did all the religious complexity and add-ons which we experience today come from? Is God impressed with our fine church buildings, doctrines, dogmas, liturgies, and ecclesiastical trappings? Is all this stuff necessary to safeguard the faith?

This is the covenant that I will make with them after those days, says the LORD: I will put My laws into their hearts, and in their minds I will write them (Hebrews 10:16).

The Accoutrements of Our Religiosity

Church history is rife with clerical ambition, greed, power grabs, and abject cruelty; even murder done in the name of this same Christ.

Does Hubert Newton's quote, and, of course, scripture like Matthew 20:25–28, have any bearing on what the *Community of the Spirit*, or, if you like, the kingdom of God should be today?

^{25}But Jesus called them to Himself and said, "You know that the rulers of the Gentiles lord it over them, and those who are great exercise authority over them.

^{26}Yet it shall not be so among you; but **whoever desires to become great among you, let him be your servant.**

^{27}**And whoever desires to be first among you, let him be your slave—**

^{28}just as the Son of Man did not come to be served, but to serve, and to give His life a ransom for many" (Matthew 20:25–28).

These comments do not mean there is no need of leadership, but it does set the tone and character of Christian leadership's role in the body of believers.

The obvious question we must ask ourselves though is: are Christ's directives or commands superseded by a later or higher cultural need or directive? After all, Christ's words were spoken over 2,000 years ago, and times have changed. Would the church have survived and succeeded with this model (that is, the greater is to serve the lesser) which Jesus gave us to follow? This model of servanthood among all members of the body is an unbreakable methodology. It is primarily the act of a servant who ministers from their own spiritual storehouse. It's called love in the Bible. Manipulation of doctrines or creedal behavior is not what Jesus did in His ministry. The top-down model is easily assuaged by oppression and elimination of the leadership. This has historically been done through oppression and persecution. The community at service to the body and the world is not easily distracted from its mission, for it is carried forth by all its participants, and its ownership is not with just the leadership. If so, that is to say, if Matthew 20:25–28 (above) had been implemented as the basic tenet of faith, how would it affect our present organizations? All of this imposition of hierarchical authority destroys the spiritual authority meant to be carried by the body and is part of spiritual and emotional baggage that we carry into the struggles of the twenty-first century church.

How do we deal with this discrepancy between what Christ directed his followers to adopt as an attitude of service and what much of the Church generally practices today? Many people of our time have just walked away from any organized religion, declaring it to be fraudulent and a sham. These sincere people often are looking for a place of expression of their faith and are left shut out, only a spectator's seat is available to them.

Sadly, many people have a higher expectation of Christian ethics than is portrayed by some leaders. Many people today, who once chose the walk of faith, have chosen to walk away from fellowship because of obvious pharisaical hypocrisy.

And as well, many have simply closed their eyes to the deficiencies of service and have found themselves a comfortable pew within the establishment. A church that has adopted the values and trappings of the current society it finds itself in just muddies the water of Christ's intent for His body of followers. No doubt when we have put our spiritual and eternal focus on the credibility of the organization that we personally follow, our confidences will be dashed when it fails to perform to expectations.

In order for Christ's mandate and His model to be workable today, must we dismantle the present system of religiosity, or is this system subject to meaningful revival and renewal? Some advocate that a convoluted system must first be broken in order to fix the system or replace it. Hopefully that is not the case.

Apparently, such renewal cannot be imposed on us from sources external to the church. Civic laws and decrees only address the external interests of the current civil laws and freedoms. Our problem is really one of the spirit and mind; our spirit and mind in these matters. Any meaningful renewal can only be generated by the actions of good men and women who seek to follow Jesus's decrees and teaching.

That, history teaches us, is precisely what has happened in the past centuries of church history. Whenever it seems that the church (establishment) becomes formalized and moribund, seeking its own pathway towards earthly glory, the Holy Spirit has a way of sidestepping the overburden of religiosity and just simply moves the real church, the *Community of the Spirit*, into another level of change, growth, and participation.

For example, as mentioned earlier, it was the corruption of the Roman Church which caused the pious Christians of that time to establish the monastic orders in the fourth to sixth centuries to get away from Rome and its decadence. These religious orders were responsible for education, universities, and the development of scientific research and a pure infant form of capitalism. A warning should be extracted from history: namely, when the church becomes overladen with its own purposes, God simply leaves it to its own devices and moves *the Community of Faith* out from under the morass. The light must shine for the lost to see and be "saved," that axiom is paramount to Christ's building of the church.

We do well to remember that Jesus said, "I will build My church" (Matthew 15:16). Mostly, Christ spoke of the coming of the kingdom of God or Heaven, and it is He who rules and reigns over its existence. He will be the final judge of all who participate in its activities (I Peter 4:5). This kingdom did not happen by expert planning of the executive church board of experts. Nor did it evolve from other religious forms of its day. His church began on the day of Pentecost and will see its ultimate consummation at His return to "catch it away" (I Thessalonians 4:16, 17). A lot of what we know now to be the Church will be left behind and tried by fire.

...each one's work will become clear; for the Day will declare it, because it will be revealed by fire; and the fire will test each one's work, of what sort it is (I Corinthians 3:13).

This church age began almost in an instant on the famous Day of Pentecost by a regenerative and empowering work of the Holy Spirit in men's hearts.

A study of the Gospels reveals the religious posture of Jesus day. It was overtly bigoted, radical, and mean-spirited. Religious leaders were ready at any presumed action of non-compliance to kill any detractors by lawful or other means. These same leaders had disenfranchised the very people who Christ met with and ministered to. These leaders considered the poor and sinful people to be outside the pale of a holy and severe God's interest.

Suddenly, the unloved and neglected became the focus of changed people's hearts as they went about providing care for material and spiritual needs. The actions taken by these folks who were changed by the energy the Holy Spirit were profoundly different than their religious culture expected or required by law.

Our passage of scripture of Acts 2 demonstrates a new ongoing model of Christian endeavor that propelled the gaze of wonderment. This same energy exists today at some level and in some manner in the churches where the Holy Spirit is active among believers. Where there are dead forms of a liturgy that looks back on past glories, this energy is obviously absent. Simply put, where the Spirit of Christ is not, the energy is not. Often men substitute form or drama in its place.

~ PART TWO ~

The 15 Notable Features of the New Community of Acts 2

Here is a rendering of Acts 2:40–47 in terms that we can analyze and apply to our Christian life in our walk of faith.

1. **Enthusiasm**

   The religion of Christ's day had degraded into a legalism that overlaid the requirements of the law with endless traditional requirements. Most of these onerous legalisms were developed during a time of captivity in Babylon. These endless obligations of sacrifice and duties brought no release or fulfillment, no joy of any stripe to their daily lives. However, Jesus declared to these captives: "If the Son makes you free, you shall be free indeed" (John 8:36).

   The breakout from Judaism's legalism brought with it an untold release of the human spirit. The many who chose Christ as Messiah experienced that Spirit grace and enthusiasm. Today the many who leave an entrenched religion of imposed duties experience release of spirit, and this grace is soon manifest as enthusiasm, vigor, and confidence for the future.

2. **Baptism**

   Today, in many religious cultures, or in cultures devoid of religion, baptism signifies a renunciation of past values and behavioral norms. Christian baptism is, in fact, a statement of faith in Christ's work of redemption. Water baptism also signifies that an important commitment to the Christian values by the candidate is being adopted through this baptism.

   Baptism is often a no-return demonstration displayed before present connections, contacts, and even family. Not only were these converts renouncing their past lifestyle but were also showing a commitment to their newly embraced Christian faith. A commitment and a choice of Jesus as Lord is made.

   There is a second, and not to be overlooked, part of this baptism ritual on the part of the *Community of Faith*. Because of the *Community of the Spirit* acting as witnesses to these baptisms, there was an implied understanding on the part of the community to undertake the receiving of the candidate into their fellowship. This commitment required a long-term work of nurturing and caring and the putting aside of prejudices.

3. **Coming together**

Community or togetherness, as a value, has its own often-unseen reward. Community is a basic need; the soul of man is in a constant search for it. Attempts to establish community is sometimes founded on unrewarding values and affinities. Some attempts, as in the case of cults and religious schisms, are quite damaging, even extremely damaging, to people's health of mind and sometimes physical being too. Often in these cases, community is perceived as conformity to the cult's established norms. Diversity and personal liberty and expression are discouraged.

Coming together as opposed to schismatic behavior, which often pervades Christian groups, is a sign that all is not well. Neither does schismatic behavior indicate that Christ's grace is at the center of the group's purposes.

The coming together of the *Community of the Spirit* makes a group attractive to searchers and is necessary for the fruit of the Spirit to flourish.

4. **Teaching**

During Jesus's earthly ministry, He took His chosen men into His confidence and taught them the mysteries and intent of the newly founded kingdom of Heaven. Once again in His teaching, contrast was noted at the heart of His discipline. This contrast with the religious customs of the day was the main reason that men became inflamed with hate. His detractors rose up against His teaching and arranged to have him crucified. Jesus fulfilled the requirements of the Law—every jot and tittle—and became the gate of righteousness by His life and death.

The new covenant He taught and invested His blood into demonstrated that the legal obligations of the law were ended. In its place, He built a convention of individual faith towards God in and through this finished work of Christ instead. Just like Abraham's faith counted to bring him into a righteous standing before God, so our faith today is the only basis or condition to achieving a righteous place before God.

The teaching of the apostle's doctrine was essential to the stabilizing and growth of the new assembly of believers. Heresy soon raised its ugly head, seeking to dilute the teaching of the apostles.

The proper teaching of truth, God's own truth, then and now, is the best antidote for error. Heresies and worldly philosophies abound and compete for the hearts and minds of believers today who seek a closer walk with Jesus.

5. **Fellowship (Participation)**

Fellowship has a distinct character of common cause. Common cause is the binder that brings people together in fellowship. In the case of the early church, the common cause was, no doubt, the resurrection of Christ and that event's eternal implications. The moral imperative of that event was the propagation of this good news, the gospel.

Redemption, as these new believers taught, was not just another ethereal expectation, but embodied the repairing of broken lives in the present time.

This "fellowship" implies participation and ownership of the cause of redemption personally. Fellowship is not a spectator sport. True fellowship, as it is worked out in the body of believers, may also readily be compared to the harmony which exists within a family.

The text of Acts 2 indicates that everyone affected was involved in some meaningful way with the work of redeeming the lives of people that they had contact with.

Today our Christian experience is often more about spectating and vicariously experiencing ministries of others, rather than personal involvement in some form of participation as a witness.

The call of Jesus to be salt and light and also to becoming a faithful witness of His work was given and directed to all believers. It was not just meant for the apostles or the generations of leaders who were to follow. Fellowship is only experienced in an active participation in a common cause. In this case, we are talking about the work of redemption and its proclamation to a lost world.

In the failure of today's Christianity to evangelize, as the command of Jesus can be understood, it is most glaringly seen in the religious stance of non-participation and un-involvement. Many authors of Christian history will attest to the energy that "every man participation" is the key to the progress of the kingdom of God.

As this task of participation was avoided and often circumscribed by the church membership, the task of being a witness of faith was taken up by the leadership. As a result, the believers soon were diminished in action to the congregation of spectators and commentators. Christianity soon changed to a control and power process exercised by the ecclesia. The work of witnessing to a lost world assumed a formal face and was soon thereafter replaced by symbolism and liturgy.

Christian fellowship today needs to be retracted from formalism towards a more vigorous personal involvement and to a revival of a *"Go ye"* endeavor.

6. Sharing of Food

The disciples of Jesus day condemned the use of precious ointment to anoint Him. They claimed, from a righteous stance, that this material could have been sold and the money used for the support of food for the poor.

The claim, however, was hypocritical because of the real teaching of the Law of Moses. The Law which these religious leaders espoused required that the ongoing daily care of the poor was a part of the generous hand to be practiced. Their general attitude towards the poor had now become a tight fist.

For the poor will never cease from the land; therefore I command you, saying, "You shall open your hand wide to your brother, to your poor and to your needy, in your land" (Deuteronomy 15:11).

Such was the gracious practice of the early church. Inclusiveness, from Moses day, just as the Law required, was the adopted practice. The people Jesus addressed in this case may not have been a homogenous lot, but they were Jewish.

Jesus's call to "whosoever will may come"[5] certainly was demonstrated in this newly formed community.

It is important to note that the Jewish Society of Jesus day was highly stratified. Sharing food in an inclusive manner was over.

The inclusive act of breaking bread together would have been seen as a radical gesture. Eating together, not just giving out as welfare, is a powerful removing of the artificial barriers of society.

When the scribes and Pharisees saw Him eating with the tax collectors and sinners, they said to His disciples, "How is it that He eats and drinks with tax collectors and sinners" (Mark 2:16)?

Such a witness of unrestricted grace and charity will bring us off of our self-imposed elevation and into the realm of sinners saved by grace. We all have need of some means of getting off of our own high

---

[5] old gospel hymn *Whosoever Will,* written by P.P. Bliss

horse. Sharing of food together in some meaningful manner, today, will help repair our damaged witness.

7. **Sharing of Possessions**

This issue doesn't seem to be a rent, loan, or borrow program. This one issue comes to the heart of our homes and bank accounts. It is both a release for us who possess things, but it also provides for the unfortunate of our society to function in a more effective manner in the challenges of life today. I have used the word release because, in so many ways, we are evaluated and "possessed" by our possessions. Often our possessions are synonymous with our identity.

Jesus taught us that those who might be fortunate enough to have two tunics ought to give one away to someone who has none, and that also applies to our food store (Luke 3:11).

We have become a society who value personal possessions to a point that we experience some level of pain at even the thought of giving up our stuff to the unfortunate. Giving our stuff away to the ones who have an honest need seems to diminish our status by its loss. Such a sense of loss is a profound witness against our cultural Christian materialism.

8. **Agreement (Concord)**

Disagreement among believers, fights, factions, and discord in churches have been a point of derision and scorn from those outside our Christian faith. To our shame, our demonstrations of the differences in passion and understanding have plagued the church throughout its long history. Whenever our common purpose of being salt and light, witnesses to a lost generation, has been overshadowed by our differences (mostly insignificant), then division is demonstrated and our effectiveness in carrying the words of redemption soon loses its appeal to the lost.

Jesus taught us how important agreement, or concord, is. Matthew 18:19 says:

"Again I say to you that if two of you shall agree on earth concerning anything that they ask, it will be done for them by My Father in heaven."

It was, no doubt, this concord, this sense of oneness, which testified against unbelief and allowed the Holy Spirit to work in their midst. Discord among brethren will always put a chill on the fires of revival. History has shown us that discord raised its ugly head again and again, to our shame.

James 3:13–16:

13Who is wise and understanding among you? Let him show by good conduct that his works are done in the meekness of wisdom.

14But if you have bitter envy and self-seeking in your hearts, do not boast and lie against the truth.

15This wisdom does not descend from above, but is earthly, sensual, demonic.

16For where envy and self-seeking exist, confusion and every evil thing are there.

Listed among the works of the flesh in Galatians 5 are "selfish ambitions, dissensions, and heresies."

How then can we think we are serving the kingdom of Heaven when these carnal issues exist among believers? Perhaps in these cases, serving the cause of our immaterial issues is more important to us than serving the cause of Christ.

How easily the body of believers could have avoided such error and loss of witness to a lost world by simply heeding the word of God.

The early church appears to have been so energized by the coming of the Holy Spirit that they were constantly in an outflow movement of grace. The inward flow of self-interest and self-aggrandizement never had a place to grow the carnal fruits of the flesh.

9. **Gladness (Good Cheer) and Simplicity**

Our referenced scripture seems to show, in Acts 2:46, that no small degree of gratitude and humility had saturated this body of new believers. This is a far cry from the mean spiritedness which often pervades a church group whose focus is on what's missing from their lives rather than what has been made available to them because of the coming of the Holy Spirit.

Nothing is more attractive to a lost world than happy people who are enjoying the provisions of a gracious God. Gladness is even contagious!

In these new believer's case, they had just been delivered from the bondage of the Law and the oppression of Jewish tradition and were experiencing a newly found spiritual freedom.

John 8:33–36 declares:

33"We are Abraham's descendants and have never been in bondage to anyone. How can you say, 'You will be made free'?"

34Jesus answered them, "Most assuredly, I say to you, whoever commits sin is a slave to sin.

35And a slave does not abide in a house forever, but a son abides forever.

36Therefore if the Son makes you free, you shall be free indeed."

And again, in Romans 8:2:

For the law of the Spirit of life in Christ Jesus has made me free from the law of sin and death.

Further gladness comes to us by abiding in this newfound freedom. Galatians 5:1 says:

Stand fast therefore in the liberty by which Christ has made us free, and do not be entangled again in a yoke of bondage.

Perhaps it is the spirit of our times or our formalized, liturgical Christianity that seems to stifle our ability to simply enjoy our blood-bought redemption. The early body of believers, lately liberated from the law of sin and death, had it together when it came to a participation of gladness and simplicity of faith in their lives. The misery of living in their times under Roman oppression would have indicated everything negative rather than the joy they displayed.

10. Worship (Praising God)

Regarding worship, isn't it a subtle thing which we experience today in our churches and Christian culture? Overt praise and worship expressed to our Savior is often seen as objectionable and even radical by the unbelieving deadweight of lukewarmness which we experience in many churches? Whereas at Pentecost, worship was an open, honest, and profound expression directed toward our Creator God; worship because of who He is and for what He has done for us.

We could benefit from visiting Isaiah 51:1:

Look to the rock from which you were hewn,

And to the hole of the pit from which you were dug.

We are not often overwhelmed today by the fact that we were doomed to hell until God extended His hand of grace to save us. He chose us and "drew us with His gentle cords of love" (Hosea 11:4). We didn't just gain salvation by some right or by reason. "[He] Jesus is the author and finisher of our faith" (Hebrews 12:2). Let gladness of heart prevail in our praise. Black shrouds and long faces will turn away honest seekers from finding true faith.

Let your light shine out towards unbelievers, but don't forget to praise God in the process. How easily, as of other things of God, praise becomes formalized and, soon, fossilized. Hopefully, in years to come, we will not have to visit a museum to discover what "Praise to God" used to look and sound like.

11. Kindness to Those Around

Suddenly the gaps and chasms of human relationships had been bridged as the fruit of the Spirit rose up in the lives of these new believers. Energized by the Holy Spirit, life looked different. They discovered a new understanding of God's intent, and people who had been estranged by sect, gender, or belief, now were not perceived as a threat. A benevolent attitude to "those around" prevailed and allowed for the transmission and communication of newly found Christian values and their possessions. This energizing force, if you will, was the winning action that brought other people to Christ. No precondition or vetting was performed; it was a case of "whoever believes":

11For the scripture says, "Whoever believes on Him will not be put to shame."

12For there is no distinction between Jew or Greek, for the same Lord over all is rich to all who call upon Him.

13For "whoever calls on the name of the LORD shall be saved" (Romans 10:11, 12, 13).

We might callously say, "So what? That was then and this is now. Life is more complex now." It's not easy to follow traditional church doctrine and to also get down to the street where people actually live out lives of pain. Mostly, however, we will find that these people we are called to are our neighbors and workmates. We "reach" them in everyday life. We even brush shoulders with them.

The contrast of the events on day one of the church were shocking; that is, the prevailing tradition and Jewish lifestyle and the energy which was displayed on this Pentecostal feast day did not easily blend. This mandate for a more generous lifestyle of religion was not a revelation, but we can see it forecast as an implicit order from God in His recorded word. Please read all of Isaiah chapter 58 to understand its full context. But for our immediate purposes, we can see this issue of generosity of Spirit commanded by God in verses 6 and 7:

6 "Is this not the fast that I have chosen:

To lose the bonds of wickedness,

To undo the heavy burdens,

To let the oppressed go free,

And that you break every yoke?

7 Is it not to share your bread with the hungry,

and that you bring to your house the poor who are cast out;

When you see the naked, that you cover him,

And hide not yourself from your own flesh?"

After all the years since Isaiah's words were recorded, Pentecost showed that the religious elite did not get it right. If they had, then the Acts 2 scenario would have passed unnoticed, déjà vu.

A further look at the prevailing behavior of that society towards the poor and dispossessed is found in the very next chapter, Acts 3. Here Peter and John are making their way to the temple to pray. Verse 2 states the case so well:

"And a certain man lame from his mother's womb was carried, whom they laid daily at the gate of the temple which is called Beautiful, to ask alms from those who entered the temple."

Isaiah 58 condemns such behavior and the Law requires that such unfortunate citizens be brought home to your house for care and sustenance. How convenient to just drop the needy off and then to depend on others for their generosity to keep him alive.

But we so often are found doing our deeds at arm's length. We just don't want to get involved with awkward causes. Jesus was often condemned for "getting down" with publicans and sinners. We have a very poor witness of Holy Spirit energized generosity in our day as well. Isaiah 58, Jesus's example, and Acts 2, combine to condemn our behavior before a righteous God.

What prevents us from getting involved with the needs of others? Is it our concern for our own security and reputation or are we like the Pharisees of Jesus day, just too good to step off our righteous platforms?

The scriptures above clearly indicate that vicarious generosity is no generosity at all if it doesn't involve our human spirit. A good question we must ask ourselves about the charity and kindness of the Community of the Spirit is: "Where have we gone wrong?" Or, "Is this model of the early church even practical today?" Has the Church forfeited the cause of kindness and charity to the State to carry and fund? Have these causes been successfully assumed by the State to the exclusion Church participation? Is that what Jesus had in mind when He taught us, "…inasmuch as you did it [charity] to one of the least of these, My brethren, you did it to Me" (Matthew 25:40).

After Constantine's approval of the church, a move was made to include the pagans in a work of charity. These Stoic pagans failed miserably in this venture as they were essentially self-seeking in their religion and not inclusive in practice. Their ventures of their sacrifices were to gain rewards for themselves. I think some of this attitude of self-seeking has crept into Christian practices today.

Note to Reader: You may wish to read the poems Passing by on the Other Side and The Woman at the Well, found in the Appendix at the back of this book.

12. Receiving New Believers

The inclusive spirit of the new Community of the Spirit was contagious and unrestricted. This was in profound contrast in an age of religious intolerance and bigotry. The whosoever will of Christ's invitation was literally worked out into the everyday function of their Christian practices. No sects, no ranking, just simply no probation, open receiving of those who came to faith in Christ. This openness is simply a standard of acceptability which the present Church is hard pressed to find in its doctrines and performance. The cry of the marginalized person's heart today is just to be accepted into a supportive fold of a caring community. How we work so hard at preventing the very thing Christ instructed us to follow, "Love one another" (1John 3:23; Matthew 22:39). We espouse God's unconditional love for sinners, but we don't readily extend an unconditional love to the unlovable.

13. Sharing (Proclaiming) the Gospel

At last, freedom from suffocating tradition and rules for every facet of life! So these believers were found to continue steadfastly teaching and receiving the apostle's doctrine. It should not come as a surprise that these new believers needed to be anchored to the truth about Christ and His finished work of redemption. And it was not very long before new gnostic heresy was being brought forth to their church to challenge the truth which they had not received.

In a world of requisite religious works, that the new believers had been freed from, a lot of confusing and aberrant teaching arose. What is notable is that these gnostic (special revelation) doctrines were not taken to the temple, but to the fledgling church in its infancy and vulnerability. Wisely, the Holy Spirit which fledged and energized the new Community of Believers also superintended the promotion and sharing of the apostle's teaching. This sharing of the apostle's doctrine provided a safeguard and a means of spiritual growth potential for the new Community of Faith. The Holy Spirit also bears witness to the truth as it is taught. In our day, most aberrant religious movements digress from the truth of the Bible and teaching about the person of Jesus as a means of establishing extra-Biblical tenets.

As a former pastor used to say, "Say what the Word says."[6] If the word of God is the final arbiter of truth, we will not easily err in our walk of faith.

14. Signs and Wonders

What made this new sect of Christian believers seem to be a viable, profound, and attractive truth? People were drawn to these new Christians primarily because of their love for each other.

This has always been the case in Christian history. Love is a sign to those who are honest seekers of God and community. But as well, the demonstration of miracles, signs, and wonders was a further demonstration of the authenticity of the Word the apostles taught.

Acts 4:33:

"And with great power the apostles gave witness to the resurrection of the Lord Jesus. And great grace was upon them all."

Hebrews 2:4:

God also bearing witness with both signs and wonders, with various miracles, and gifts of the Holy Spirit, according to His own will.

The resurrection power of Jesus was evident among this band of new believers, and it was manifest proof of the credibility of the teaching of the apostles. It further demonstrated that the work of the Holy Spirit was genuine.

Throughout Christian history, there have been manifestations of signs and wonders which have also given credibility to the truth preached as people turned their affections towards God.

However, too often, signs and wonders are taken as an affirmation of the evangelist's credibility and not the true teaching of the Word of God. Distortions of this sort always end up in the discrediting of the work of God. Men soon follow men, lay aside the Word of God, and cling to the words of men. How often we seem to get it all backwards. Many "signs and wonders" ministries fail to include other aspects of the original plan for the church. They soon become a Johnny one-note plan. The unsaid lesson is that this aspect is the better choice as a witnessing tool. These ministries soon become about the "favor of God" on the leader instead of an outflow of love to the world. Again, let it be said, this Day of Pentecost package of God's outpouring

---

[6] Rev. J.C. O'Brien, pastor of Gospel Centre Church (Edmonton, Alberta) from 1955–1972

cannot be cherry picked. Church leaders need to understand that they are all (15 features) needed to establish a full credibility to the lost.

15. Prayer

Prayer, the simple expression of faith's desires directed towards a caring God.

Prayer has been variously described by some as a desperate reaching towards a distant God or an expression of our base wishes directed towards an unknown force.

We have library shelves stocked with books defining how to pray effectively, how to pray to make our wishes realized, or even the most meaningful words to use in effective prayer.

The Acts 2 community seemed to pray instinctively as they were prompted by the Holy Spirit. They seemed to understand the meaning of Luke 18:1, "men always ought to pray and not lose heart"; and 1 Thessalonians 5:17, "pray without ceasing."

- They prayed for the sick to recover;
- they prayed for adequate resources to carry on day to day living (daily bread);
- they prayed for safety;
- they prayed in the Spirit and
- they prayed with their understanding (1 Corinthians 14:15).

Prayer was not seen as a sidebar issue or a last resort action.

Simply put, prayer was woven into the fabric of their everyday lives.

Prayer was an essential feature of the Community of the Spirit in every way.

The prayer of faith makes the other fourteen (14) features mentioned earlier both workable and effective; oil for the machinery as it were.

Prayer binds us to God and His workings in our life.

When we resist praying as a proper part of our Christian experience, any number of distractions will occupy our interest and our time.

Simple prayers are as effective as profound words if they are expressed in faith.

Prayer can quietly resolve major problems or shake the prisons which are not of our own making (Acts 5:19), a case of a physical prison. And Matthew 8:28–33 states the case of two demonically imprisoned Gadarenes.

The Bible is full of instructions about prayer:

"Ask and it shall be given you" (Matthew 7:7).

"...how much more will your heavenly Father give good things to those who ask Him" (Matthew 7:11)?

"And whatever things you ask in prayer, believing, you will receive" (Matthew 21:22).

"Until now you have asked nothing in My name. Ask and you will receive that your joy may be full" (John 16:24).

~Prayer is not the influential prevue of the holy.

~Prayer is the effective resource of the sanctified.

~Prayer is the oxygen of the Community of the Spirit.

~~~~~

We are not so much instructed how to pray,

or when to pray,

but we are instructed just to pray—always.

~ PART THREE ~

Returning to Our Roots

The intention of this commentary is not to say that there is a need to develop new dogmas or rituals or theology, but simply to try to return to the origin of our Christian faith and to examine the witness of its profound beginning.

This unique beginning of values and energy propelled the infant church forwards through centuries of persecution and opposition.

It may come as somewhat of a surprise to us today to learn that Christ did not come to earth with the expressed intent of creating a new religion. He came to establish the kingdom of God. The New Testament is our constitution and mandate. Look what the centuries of ambitious churchmen have made of His work.

Erasmus (1466–1536) stated: "…for He is concerned with religion as a worship from the heart, that has no need of the offices and intermediaries supplied by the Church." True religion, Erasmus insists, is a form of folly in the sense that it is simplistic and direct, not convoluted with unnecessary sophistications and dogmatic doctrine.

The quest for an original faith presents us with the question of our present practices and values at play in the church today.

The questions to be asked are:

Are the tenets and practices of the established church today merely adaptations of pagan practices and values?

And has some degree of these original tenets been retained and adapted to our denominational goals?

Most of these questionable practices and values were brought to the Church after it was overrun by the unregenerate sons of Roman nobility. This occurred as the Roman government *captured* the church for its own purposes and came as a result of Constantine's approval of the Roman Church.

Instead of a vibrant faith practiced by all the Christians, a liturgical practice, dramatized by the priests who, in doing so, took the participation by the believers away from them. The masses of sincere believers were left to become idle spectators of representative Christianity instead of vital participants.

Perhaps we should examine our present-day faith practice:

Are our faith and values a reflection of our current cultural norms?

Is it not of some importance that our Christian faith, born on Pentecost, should never become a reflection of our acceptable cultural norms?

When was the culture of the world ever a friend and ally of the kingdom of God?

Does true Christian faith always assault cultural norms?

And, perhaps, if it is authentic; should it not do so?

This culturally accepted Church of Rome soon began to exalt and promote itself at the expense of piety. They began to assimilate the pagan faith of nations, states, and pagan groups into their folds by baptizing the leadership of such groups and then declaring that all the nation or state had become Christian through these fraudulent baptismal actions. No real change of heart was affected by their actions except that the Romans overlaid their dogmas and ritual on the people who were *assumed* into the fold. These people still retained their folk religions and practices, their idols, their superstitions, and feast day celebrations. To date, many nations proclaim to be Christian but allow and promote worship of folk idols and faith in amulets.

Many pagan "saints" and heroes, some long dead, were baptized into the fold and given a Roman "Saint" designation and feast day. However clever the Romans thought they were, they did not change the heart of the common man. Neither did these unregenerate new Romans change their hearts or add anything of value to the kingdom of God. The Roman *Church of Power* benefited by this exchange with increased political power and often inflated incomes which were realized as a direct result of imposed tithes and offerings.

The Church in Action

The earlier Christian church had limited political power and governance. Despite that limitation, it propelled its phenomenal growth into all the areas around the Mediterranean Sea. No hierarchy to politicize its practices was available, only an elected local bishop (overseer) and lesser offices of deacons and elders were in place to teach and to serve an active body of believers. These believers were all active *salt and light* witnesses of the gospel to a corrupted and oppressed population.

In the first century, and repeatedly a century later, major outbreaks of plague attacked the population around the Mediterranean Sea. History records several major plague outbreaks covering the area of Europe, Asia, and North

Africa. Of these, the plague of 165–180 AD caused the loss of an estimated 30% of the population. Another major plague occurred from 250–266 AD with similar loss of life. Many other plague outbreaks of various diseases and severity occurred which were not as wide spread as these major ones.

These plagues, involving such a great loss of life, decimated the population groups of the region giving distinction to the Christian population. Although reviled and often persecuted, these authentic Christians stepped up with basic care and nursing and, in the process, showed Christianity for its true nature in the practical things of everyday life.

At the first sign of sickness in a region affected, the patient was removed from the house by fearful pagan family and left at the roadside to die, perhaps a fearful but pragmatic practice. The Christians, however, exercised compassion on the afflicted and did not follow this practice of abandonment but chose to nurse the sick back to health using basic patient care. Often the Christians took the abandoned pagan sick into their own homes and nursed them back to health also. The Christian survival rates, even given that some caregivers were also infected, were much higher than the pagans who lived near them.

This witness to the pagans of the vitality of the Christian faith caused many to convert to Christianity as a superior life choice. This witness was seen in their charity and pure lifestyle as well as their confidence in God's providence for their lives. Often the reply to Christian practices was, "See how they love each other," (Tertullian, 160–225 AD).

Leo Tolstoy, in his work *A Confession*[7], says it so well,

"The church's perversion of Christianity has distanced us from the realization of the kingdom of God"; but Christian truth, like fire on dry wood, has consumed the outer layer and burst forth. Everyone can see the significance of Christianity and its influence is already stronger than the deceit which conceals it.

The perversion that has diluted Christianity from its true cause and effectiveness was the Roman Church's lust for power and supremacy and its unscrupulous drive by (often-unchristian) men as they sought to regain the glory of the waning Roman Empire through its terror and politics. One of the early evidences of this motive in action was the establishment of the Holy Roman Empire in Europe. It was established by the Roman church as it exercised an extremely perverted authority over kings and rulers and the masses of ignorant peasants using the threat of excommunication and the revolt of the realm's subjects who were still loyal to the Roman rulers. So, often, as

---

[7] Leo Tolstoy, *A CONFESSION and other Religious Writings*, (Penguin Books, 1987)

the church attempts to establish the kingdom of God on earth through political means, it perverts Christ's cause.

The Heart of the Matter

Much of what we know of religion (the outward appearance) anywhere and anytime is the result of human reason and not revelation. The coming of the Holy Spirit on the Day of Pentecost brought with it a new revelation about the population's relationship to God and its obligation to their fellowmen. It took the wisdom of the first apostles who lived close to Christ to document this knowledge of the teaching of Christ and the application of this Pentecostal experience into the New Testament. This revelation is provided for us in the Bible, the written Word of God. However, we still struggle to discover, understand, and apply it to our hearts and practices in a pure form today.

Even as the infant church was being expanded into the Gentile populations away from Jerusalem, the nature of this new revelation was primarily spiritual, not political or religious in any sense. That spiritual force was its unbeatable force which paganism could not compete with.

The direction of the New Testament provides very little formal instruction in how we are to govern others, but it does provide much useful information on how to govern our own hearts.

The heart is the real heart of the matter.

Read and contemplate Colossians 3:1–25. It provides information on how Christians are to interact for the benefit of all. Of note are verses 12–17:

[12]Therefore, as the elect of God, holy and beloved, put on tender mercies, kindness, humility, meekness, longsuffering;

[13]bearing with one another, and forgiving one another, if anyone has a complaint against another; even as Christ forgave you, so you also must do.

[14]But above all things put on love, which is the bond of perfection.

[15]And let the peace of God rule in your hearts, to which also you were called in one body; and be thankful.

[16]Let the word of Christ dwell in you richly in all wisdom, teaching and admonishing one another in psalms and hymns and spiritual songs, singing with grace in your hearts to the Lord.

[17]And *whatsoever* you do in word or deed, *do* all in the name of the Lord Jesus, giving thanks to God the Father through Him.

Notice how devoid of specific requisite tasks, rank, hierarchy, and political consideration this passage of scripture is. Simply put, all this applies equally to all of us, all the time, and in all cases.

This directive is pointed at all believers and readily fits with the Acts 2 response to the coming of the Holy Spirit. Here are the directives of Colossians 3:12–17 working out practically how the initial enthusiasm prevents our behavior and attitude from going astray. This scripture reference is not unlike the spirit of the sermon Jesus delivered on the mountain in Galilee (Matthew 5, 6, 7).

Contrasts and Conflicts

There is an arrogant state of mind in the Church today that seems to indicate that the established model of today is superior to the primitive model shown in Acts 2. This argument ignores the fact that the more developed model has lost most of the meaningful values and energy which were birthed at Pentecost.

This present state of mind raises a conflict and a question: "Whose church is it anyway?"

Do those who call themselves the participants in the church today have the right to change the basic Biblical tenets, purposes, and practices that the Holy Spirit appears to have put in place to grow the kingdom of God?

How does today's practice of Christianity compare with the intent of the Holy Spirit on Pentecost?

Or does any of this matter at all if we are just sincere?

Do we conduct Christian service to satisfy our own goals and purposes?

Is cultural relativity what we need to strive for?

The primitive model is often best displayed or observed in third world countries or among some breakaway ministries.

Jesus said, "**I will** build My church, and the gates of Hades shall not prevail against it" (Matthew 16:18).

He referenced His church (body), the whole company of believers or congregation, not an institution.

His building plan—not ours!

The church of self-seeking ends seems to be well portrayed in the work of Dostoevsky, *The Brothers Karamazov*.[8] In this classic presentation, the Cardinal arrests Jesus and speaks derisively to Him about His temporary return

---

[8] Fyodor Dostoevsky, *THE BROTHERS KARAMAZOV, the Constance Garnett Translation revised by Ralph E. Matlaw*, (W.W. Norton & Company, Inc., 500 Fifth Avenue, N.Y. 10110, 1976) 227–245.

to earth. The setting of this parable is the time of the Spanish Inquisition. The chapter called "The Grand Inquisitor" was reflecting the time of persecution of heretics about the sixteenth century (1500s). Although this is a work of fiction, it perhaps is driven by a prevailing truth.

(The underlines in the following quotes are by author for the purpose of emphasis.)

The Cardinal further challenges Jesus with this insolent charge: "The church was yours and you gave it to the Pope. There is no need for you to come now and interfere. You gave the people freedom of faith (emphasis added), and they could not handle the conscience that went with that gift."

He continues, "We [the Roman Church] have persuaded the people to come and 'lay down' your freedom of faith at our feet! In exchange, we have given them miracle, mystery, and authority (emphasis added), and the people are happy to not have to deal with their conscience." (abridged)

We so readily assign the blame of substitution and usurpation of the golden provision of Pentecost with the leaden provisions provided today in the Roman church. However, historically and presently, the Protestant faith is not void of substitution and usurpation either by disingenuous practices, dogmas, and liturgy in our modern churches. In many areas of church institutionalism in our own regimes, the genuine faith, like that of the early church, has been replaced by ordinances which smack of "miracle, mystery, and authority." We all know that to be true, but we rationalize our actions as being a necessary or convenient work for the betterment of the Church. It's not just that we substitute the gold with lead, but we seem to feel justified by our measured successes in doing so.

Did the Roman Church teach us the game of substitution of the real by the disingenuous?

The Christian revelation that Jesus demonstrated and which the Holy Spirit inspired, was recognized as the principle espousing the equality of men; that is, that God is our Father and that all men are brothers (Matthew 12:48). This tenet struck to the core of the monstrous tyranny which overshadowed the known civilized world of that time. This good news soon smashed the slaves' chains and annihilated the enormous injustice which allowed a small privileged group of people to live in luxury at the expense and by the effort of the subjugated masses. The so-called lower classes were ill-treated and exploited by the attitudes of that day and the centuries which followed.

This conflict of ideals was one of the prime reasons why the first Christians were persecuted. Once it became clear that the influence exerted by the Church, regarding morals and the issues of faith, could not be suppressed, the ruling classes adopted this energy and perverted it and subjected it to serve their own ambitions.

True Christianity ceased to be the celebration of the first centuries and, to a significant extent, became the tool of the privileged classes.

The following is quoted by Tolstoy in his work *The Law of Love and The Law of Violence*[9]:

In 1682 in England, Doctor Laytian, an honorable gentleman who wrote a book against the Episcopate, was judged and sentenced to the following punishment: he was cruelly flogged, his ear was then sliced off, one half of his nose was split, and then the initials for "Disseminator of Trouble" were branded on his cheek with a hot iron. Seven days later, he was flogged again, and although the scars had not yet healed, the other side of his nose was split, the other ear was sliced off, and the other half of his cheek was branded. All this was done in the name of Christianity. (John Morrison Davidson)

These heinous acts were not an isolated case, but have been repeated by the ruling clerical class against dissenters who longed to see the practice of the original faith of Pentecost brought forth in their day. A very long list of ecclesiastically raised charges upon discontented and honorable men resulted in beatings, imprisonment, burnings, drawings, etc. continued throughout the centuries. You may recall the accounts by John Foxe in *Foxes Book of Martyrs* (first published in England by John Day in 1563) or John Bunyan's tale *The Pilgrims Progress* (first published in England 1673).

The law of love (James 2:8) instituted by Christ and understood to be the supreme law of humanity was acknowledged as a basic tenet of Christianity, but it was not applied to the everyday practice of life. It has often been idolized as a cause of Christ. It was never given a full or proper place in Church dogma or civil law.

It seems to be quite apparent that when men begin to try to build the kingdom of Heaven on earth by political, self-serving means, the true faith falls into form and dogma and lacks the personal and internal energy to bear the fruit of the Bible model.

Tolstoy, in his book, *A Confession*, states:

But the Christian teaching in its true meaning, recognizing the law of love as supreme and permitting no exceptions in its application to life ruled out any form of violence and, consequently, could not but condemn the whole structure of the world founded on violence. And this chief significance of the teaching was hidden from people by false Christianity.[10]

---

[9] Leo Tolstoy, *A CONFESSION and other Religious Writings*, (Penguin Books, 1987), 151

[10] Leo Tolstoy, *A CONFESSION and other Religious Writings*, (Penguin Books, 1987), 175

We may rightly ask ourselves the question: what is the importance of a universal application of the *Community of the Spirit* model today? After all, we are not poor peasants; here in the western world, do we not enjoy profound material success?

It is often said, however, that the spiritual condition of this western church is a mile wide and an inch deep. That is, it looks vast, but it is not strong enough to withstand persecution from its opponents or contamination from the world it is sent to save. Christianity that is culturally dependent is itself in jeopardy.

Often our methods of self-evaluation and affirmation are not so very different from the world's methodology. We look good in our own eyes, so did the men of the Good Samaritan parable (Luke 10:33–36).

(Please see the poem *Passing by on the Other Side* in the Appendix.)

We adhere to the concept of assimilation rather than replacement. True light and salt do not assimilate, they replace darkness and apply lifesaving preservation and taste.

The Roman Church, which was provided an enormous amount of support and legitimacy by the State, attracted many insincere candidates who set about re-establishing the fading glory of the empire. It exercised a fraudulent authority wrested from scripture and utilized the strengths and appeal of the Christian church (Matthew 16:18, 19). What happened next was an opening of the floodgates of ambition, greed, and a lust for power, all in the Church's name.

If the early infant church is an appropriate model, then Biblical outcomes and the fulfillment of the Lord's directives can be our only measure of success, as Jesus stated in Luke 17:20–21:

[20]Now when He was asked by the Pharisees when the kingdom of God would come, He answered them and said, "The kingdom of God does not come with observation;

[21]nor will they say, See here! or See there! For indeed, the kingdom of God is within you."

We can never justify the application of carnal precepts, which the ungodly ascribe to, as a means or measure of the Church's success. It has deadly results and can never be used to achieve any Godly goals.

How easily we stumble over the simplicity of such Biblical statements. We are caught up with the notion that our Christian efforts ought to be visible and played out before a worldly audience. Indeed, we are like the Old Testament Israelites who longed to be like other nations and peoples around them. They assumed, in many cases, the lifestyle and idols of their pagan neighbors. God was not so politically correct. He called it adultery. The results were catastrophic as they gained God's disapproval and punishment for their waywardness.

Tertullian, about the year 160 AD, said of the Christian church who still labored under terrible persecution by Roman and local authorities: "We are but of yesterday, and we have filled all your places—cities, islands, forts, towns, market places, and forums. We have left nowhere to you except the temples of your gods."

This is Christian progress and success; unseen, perhaps, but the effects were visible in the behavior of the affected individuals.

It appears, from a Biblical perspective, that our programs, our financial numbers, and our attendance figures pale before the imperative of the church's calling; or more clearly, the kingdom's mandate of being a valid witness of salt and light to a dying and lost world.

Stark, in his book *Cities of God* [1], states:

Although the very first Christian converts in the West [of Israel, not Syria, Iraq etc.] may have been by fulltime missionaries, the conversion process soon became self-sustaining as new converts accepted the challenge to spread their faith and did so by missionizing their immediate circle of intimates. This offended many pagans and has confused some historians. Pagans saw something sinister in "the personal approaches made by some Christians to non-Christians." As for the historians, three of the most prominent recent historians[2] of religions in the Roman Empire find it surprising that Christianity continued to grow after Paul, as there seems to have been no organized or systematic program attracting non-believers. Whereas it may have lacked a bureaucratic structure or systematic programming, personal evangelism was the program.

Rodney Stark[11]

The western churches have erred through the centuries, and continue on that track, in that we have supplanted the "program" of personal involvement and personal evangelism by replacing it with formalizing the very effective heritage passed to us by the early church.

Formalization has also shifted the operation of evangelization from the re-born to the artificially created hierarchy which mimics the Old Testament regime. It has created a professional class of functionaries and has de-legitimized the witness of the Christian masses, the *Community of the Spirit.*

---

[11] Rodney Stark, *CITIES OF GOD, The Real Story of How Christianity Became an Urban Movement and Conquered Rome* (Harper Collins Publishers, New York, NY 10022, 2006), 14,15; [2 notes] Beard, North and Price Chapter One Notes 41 & 42

Formalization of the faith has brought with it dogma, liturgy, ritual, symbolism, and more importantly, the lack of responsiveness to the opportunity of ministry by the saints to their pagan neighbors.

This formalization has taken on very attractive and regal forms which, in effect, are part of the "gilded bushel" that hides the true light of Christ's gospel.

You will recognize from several Biblical passages that Christ never chose the mighty to overwhelm the lesser levels of men and women. The Commission of "Go ye into all the world and preach the gospel" was given to all believers (Luke 9:60). This change of activity and roles came directly from Rome's overt action to take control of the church after Constantine.

Given the monopoly situation (Constantine), the privileged Christian clergy were content to recreate a church very similar to the subsidized temple religions of ancient civilizations, especially in terms of ignoring the religious need of the general public. They were so lacking in energy that it took many centuries to expand the Church beyond the old boundaries of the Roman Empire, and even then, the "Christianization" of the north amounted to little more than becoming the monopoly state population un-missionized. (Rodney Stark[12])

The Saints

The growth of the post-Constantine Church produced numerous semi-pagans and non-authentic "Christians" as a result of indiscriminate or ingenuous baptisms of various leaders of states. These newly created Churchmen exercised a newfound control over the leaders of these states as a result of the Churches distorted doctrine of authority.

The masses of the population in these baptized states were left un-evangelized, unconverted, and untaught. For the most part, life continued on as they retained much of their pagan folk superstition and their idols.

The long dead pagan folk heroes, or "saints," were often consecrated beginning in the fourth century and continuing into the eighth (400 AD to 800 AD), and their worship of the pagan "saints" was not disrupted as Rome continued its control of the ignorant masses.

(The underlines in the following quotes of scripture are by author for the purpose of emphasis.)

I Samuel 2:9 states, "He will guard the feet of His saints."

But the saints of the Most High shall receive the kingdom, and possess the kingdom forever, even forever and ever (Daniel 7:18).

---

[12] Rodney Stark, *DISCOVERING GOD* (Harper One, 2007), 329

2 Chronicles 6:41 implores God:

"Now therefore,

Arise, O LORD God, to Your resting place,

You and the ark of Your strength.

Let Your priests, O LORD God,

Be clothed with salvation,

And let Your saints rejoice in goodness."

The New Testament continues this theme:

And the graves were opened; and many bodies of the saints who had fallen asleep were raised (Matthew 27:52).

To all who are in Rome, beloved of God, called *to be* saints:

Grace to you and peace from God our Father and the Lord Jesus Christ (Romans 1:7).

"Now He who searches the heart knows what the mind of the Spirit is, because He makes intercession for the saints according to *the will of* God" (Romans 8:27).

The designation of "saints" should not be considered to be too ethereal or as the prerogative of religious clerics. This concept is tied to the here and now in the following two verses:

25But now I [Paul] am going to Jerusalem to minister to the saints.

26For it pleased those from Macedonia and Achaia to make a certain contribution for the poor among the saints who are in Jerusalem (Romans 15:25 & 26).

…when He comes, in that Day, to be glorified in His saints and to be admired among all those who believe (2 Thessalonians 1:10).

Simply put, the saints are earthbound believers who are "sanctified" by their faith in the redeeming work of Christ. "Saints" means "sanctified ones," a simple and profound work of the Holy Spirit, not the prevue of the ecclesia.

The Roman Church has created a special status for dead churchmen and women who lived commendable lives on earth, and these men and women as "Saints" are considered to be holy enough by this designation to intercede with God on our behalf. The Bible, however, plainly declares:

24But He [Jesus Christ], because He continues forever, has an unchanging priesthood.

25Therefore He is also able to save to the uttermost those who come to God through Him, since He always lives to make intercession for them (Hebrews 7:25).

He is the Intercessor, He makes intercession, not the long dead "Saints."

So it is that the Roman Church has developed a special status for redeemed sinners who have been saved by God's grace and not by their own virtue. This making of saints is no more than the practice by the ecclesiastics of continuing the practice of the Roman Empire's Senate in declaring "Worthy" Caesars to be divine and to be worshiped; the ridiculous inferring of the divine upon the dead by the profane.

The only credible designation of "intercessor" before God's holy throne was given in the Bible to Jesus, the only one worthy of such honor.

The platform before the Lord's throne has always been flat and lowly. There never were any elevated positions of advantage. We are all just sinners saved by His grace.

Worship and praise are to be reserved for Him alone. Despite the theology that directs people to pray to the elevated saints, who were created by profane men, Biblical references give no cause or permission to create such elevated saints; quite the reverse is true, "See that thou worship not me…" (Revelation and other places). Church titles alone do not bestow holiness upon those who live and serve in manmade churches. It is a fraudulent process and practice. And yet churchmen continue to name churches, holidays, and institutions after the "sainted" men and women. These created "saints" are no more better saints than the people you will sit next to in church next Sunday. It is farcical to do otherwise than what the Bible directs us to understand as we live and pray before a just and gracious God.

Reaching the Lost

Personal evangelism is a trendy word so often used in Christian programs today. It is often a hard sell to motivate Christians of the everyday type, that is, the non-professionals, to carry out the ministry of reconciliation into the marketplace and into family gatherings. This problem probably has two main causes.

As mentioned earlier, beginning with Constantine's approval of the Christian religion and the hijacking of its governance by power hungry professionals, the ownership of ministry tasks was coveted by the Roman clerics and restricted to the selected "ordained."

Dedicated evangelists, of the everyday stripe and who were not professionals, were soon disenfranchised by the addition of mystery and authoritative levels of the ministry previously carried out by the sincere, motivated believers as simple works of charity and service. This presumptive deed was completed by assuming authority by formally establishing the scriptures already in use as the Canon and then establishing extra-Biblical doctrine and dogma as tradition. Clerics also worked extensively to prevent access to the scriptures by anyone but their "anointed" priests. It is interesting to find that, in New Testament times, the only "Anointed One" was Jesus. Otherwise the anointing we **all** have is internal and of the Holy Spirit, "but the anointing which you have received from Him abides in you" (I John 2:27). Again, the status which has been established as "professional" and "non-professional" believers is not supported by scripture. There is no case for us to make the status of sinners an "us and them." The only just division based on holiness is "us and Him."

Access to heaven was assumed as the warrant of the priests, and then access to God's grace was fraudulently taken away from the simple act of faith in the Word of God.

For by grace you have been saved through faith, and that not of yourselves; *it is* the gift of God (Ephesians 2:8).

The masses of those seeking access to God were left to be utterly dependent on the priesthood for access to God's blessing. The priesthood wrongly taught that they alone held the keys to heaven and entry into the kingdom provisions was dependent on the exercise of the priestly discretion.

People readily fell into a state of blind, ignorant obedience and soon behaved like sheep in need of a benevolent shepherd.

This assumed authority, and its challenges made to this false state by men of the Spirit and conscience, was the cause for much of the persecution and heretic burning which followed into the centuries which followed.

To this date, we have not yet returned to the vigor of the infant church in pursuit of our *salt and light* witness to a lost world. Too readily we, the congregants who were initially charged with the salt and light task, have abdicated our position in preference and deference and privilege to the professionals.

It must be plainly stated that, often, the professionals love their positions of deference and are quick to defend it. Ministry, regardless of how ineffective it might be, is not easily given away to the people of the church. These people, however, are the very ones Jesus so often spoke to about becoming His witnesses or, at the least, they were included with the apostles in His commands to "go and witness."

At its root, this imbalance or inconsistency in today's church is more of a legacy problem than of structure. The presumed model and the practice of governance that was developed post-Constantine is still philosophically and overtly in place to some extent in Protestant churches today.

Church councils still, today, sit in judgment of the faith and behavior of individuals. These councils still impose their conclusions against dissenters and malefactors as to the appropriately deemed chastisement and estrangement. These judgments are used as a ready means of achieving conformance and subjection to authority. These actions are overt issuances of judgment, just as the Roman Church practiced. However severe these judgments are, they cannot exceed the civil law or constitutional provisions of the state today. In severe judgments, the Church of the past simply passed the guilty over to the state to exercise physical punishment, even to the use of the death penalty.

Correction and restoration of those in error was, in Bible times, a function of the body of spiritual men.

Brethren, if a man is overtaken in any trespass, you who *are* spiritual restore such a one in a spirit of gentleness, considering yourself lest you be tempted (Galatians 6:1).

~ PART FOUR ~

The Militant Church

After departing from a mindset of religious duties and practices, a vacuum of responsibilities and purpose may soon have occurred with the early church. At that time, the Ten Commandments of the Law of Moses were soon found to be overtaken by the Two Commandments of Jesus:

[37]Jesus said to him, "*You shall love the LORD your God with all your heart, with all your soul, and with all your mind.*"

[38]This is the first and the great commandment.

[39]And *the* second *is* like it: "*You shall love your neighbor as yourself*" (Matthew 22:37–39).

The first charge to the church of these newly born Christians was for individual believers to demonstrate a vital love for the Lord and, as scripture directs, "with all the understanding, with all the soul, and with all the strength" (Mark 12:33).

Secondly, they were instructed "to love their neighbors as themselves" (Mark 12:33) as was demonstrated in Acts 2:40–47 and again in Acts 4:32–37; that is, they shared their store of food and possessions.

Jesus also gave the community of believers a mandate to "go into all the world and preach the gospel to every creature" (Mark 16:15). The nature of this *going* is realized in the zeal and lack of fear or personal risk that was practiced. This is where we find this community of believers demonstrating an evangelical militancy for the first time. From a depressed and disenfranchised people, they were fired up and aggressive in their newly found compassion and message of hope.

The armed conflicts and bloodshed that followed from the fourth (300 AD) to sixteenth (1500 AD) centuries was a demonstration of religious ambition for the so-called *cause of Christ*. However, it was more about pride, dogma, personal threat, power and prestige, and wealth and control than about "loving your neighbor as yourself." None of these aforementioned elements of prestige were at issue with the newborn Church of Pentecost. For example, while men built great churches to the "glory of God," multitudes died of starvation and deprivation. This perversion of values does not reflect the Acts 2 model of charity.

This newborn church was ushered in with a zero balance on their spiritual or moral merit ledgers. But they were given a mandate of "bearing much fruit" (John 15:8) and "walking in the Spirit" (Galatians 5:16).

The hard question today for this community to meet Christ's direction is obviously: was this infant church capable of producing the fruit of the Spirit without the superstructure of an "organization," the Establishment which was later overlaid on church ministries in the centuries to follow?

In fact, there is a lack of evidence that the Church of Establishment has ever produced the fruit of the Spirit. Only the body of true believers is capable of satisfying Christ's call of fruitfulness as directed in Galatians 5:22–26:

[22]But the fruit of the Spirit is love, joy, peace, longsuffering, kindness, goodness,

[23]gentleness, self-control. Against such there is no law.

[24]And those *who are* Christ's have crucified the flesh with its passions and desires.

[25]If we live in the Spirit, let us also walk in the Spirit.

[26]Let us not become conceited, provoking one another, envying one another.

This fourth century *pile on* effect of the ecclesia hobbled the infant church, causing it to lose its vitality and focus. This overburden changed their focus from a service of faith and devotion to the Lord as a vital witness of salt and light, to a service to the ecclesia and their newly pronounced dogmas and their unauthorized governance. Matthew 20:25–28 provides a clear judgment on those who seek the over-lordship of believers:

[25]But Jesus called them to *Himself* and said, "You know that the rulers of the Gentiles lord it over them, and those who are great exercise authority over them,

[26]Yet it shall not be so among you; but whoever desires to become great among you, let him be your servant.

[27]And whoever desires to be first among you, let him be your slave.

[28]just as the Son of Man did not come to be served, but to serve, and to give His life a ransom for many."

Martin Bucer (born 1491), the true father of Calvinism, summarized the tasks of pastoral care in this manner:

a. To seek and to find all the lost.
b. To bring back those that are scattered.
c. To heal the wounded.
d. To strengthen the sickly.
e. To protect the healthy and to put them to pasture.

In a standard vineyard, unless care is taken, the vine will grow along the ground, and the fruit will be destroyed. Trellises are constructed and situated in a manner to allow the fruit to grow prudently and produce mature fruit for the harvest. The trellis produces no fruit of its own, only the living vine can produce fruit. So the structure of the Establishment should be in place in a manner which will allow the proper growth of the vine to fruitfulness. No matter what the complexity and the beauty of the trellis, the fruit is still born by the vine.

Jesus taught us not to hide our light under a bushel because we, the church, are the light of the world; or perhaps we can say the light to the world (Matthew 5:13–16):

[13]You are the salt of the earth; but if the salt loses its flavor, how shall it be seasoned? It is then good for nothing but to be thrown out and trampled underfoot by men.

[14]You are the light of the world. A city that is set on a hill cannot be hidden.

[15]Not do they light a lamp and put it under a basket, but on a lampstand, and it gives light to all *who are* in the house.

[16]Let your light so shine before men, that they may see your good works and glorify your Father in heaven.

In every country, since Jesus ascended to heaven, this light has raised the hope and aspirations, and the achievements of nations, by showing that there is a better way to live. Conversely, wherever the gospel has been refused, human rights and aspirations have been blunted. The world we seek to assist often refuses Christ's light to their own detriment. The darkness of the world systems, which inhabits the unbeliever's soul, has tried to push back against this light. However, we are likened to a city set on a hill; the light on a hill is not easily obscured.

In so many (too many) instances in history, the *Community of the Spirit* has allowed themselves to be intimidated by false ideas and values raised by a culture of unbelievers and ambitious men. These false values and ideas do not help to shine the light into the dark places in men's hearts. We have even, at times, admired and applauded these false ideas, values, and issues raised by the unbelieving culture and which obviously hide the light.

These things are comparable to gilding the very bushel which hides the true treasure, the true light. The militant church of our day must find effective ways to avoid becoming overloaded with the unfruitfulness of the gilded bushel and the trellis. We must put an urgent *"Go!"* into our calling as individuals in Christ Jesus. We must each search our hearts in these matters and correct our values and actions.

To a large part, many of the churches today have enjoyed the mesmerizing distractions of the ritual and liturgy of church services. Often, they are performed for the express purpose of elevating their own establishment's credibility and vested authority, not Christ's kingdom. The *feel-good* sense about ourselves that follows these church activities does not address the Laodicea castigation which should truly represent our personal state and personal causes (Revelation 3:14–22).

Because you say, "I am rich, have become wealthy, and have need of nothing" and do not know that you are wretched, miserable, poor, blind, and naked (Revelation 3:17).

How the first century church would rise up and condemn our feeble self-congratulatory efforts at the advancement and participation of the kingdom of God that Jesus came to establish.

Colossians 1:9–13 informs us that this New Testament church must be "worthy of the Lord" who shed His blood to establish it.

[9]For this reason we also, since the day we heard it, do not cease to pray for you, and to ask that you be filled with the knowledge of His will in all wisdom and spiritual understanding;

[10]that you may walk worthy of the Lord, fully pleasing to *Him*, being fruitful in every good work and increasing in the knowledge of God;

[11]strengthened with all might, according to His glorious power, for all patience and longsuffering with joy

[12]giving thanks to the Father who has qualified us to be partakers of the inheritance of the saints in the light.

[13]He has delivered us from the power of darkness and conveyed *us* into the kingdom of the Son of His love,

So, we see that the Church is to be:
- Fully pleasing to Him,
- Fruitful in good works,
- Increasing in knowledge of God (know the Lord),
- Strengthened with all might,
- According to His glorious power,
- Patient and longsuffering…with joy.
- Giving thanks to the Father.
- Qualified for the inheritance of the saints…in light.
- He has delivered us from the power of darkness and
- Conveyed us into the kingdom of the Son of His love.

Focus on Values

Four notable values or principles should earmark the identification and the function of our New Testament churches today, if we are to be called authentic. They are:

1. **Christ alone must be glorified** in the community by its works.
2. Everything invented or developed as ministry should be designed for **the common good**.
3. The Holy Spirit and His provisions are **not for personal** consumption. Empowered to serve.
4. All members of the *Community of the Spirit* are meant to function spiritually. **"Go ye all."**

The questions we can legitimately raise are:

Does the *Community of the Spirit*, as it is found today, contain the necessary energy and the Godly wisdom required to propel itself forward in a sinful, threatening world; or,

Does the overburden of the organization it serves under suppress the expression of such energy?

Does the *Firm* own the body?

In doing so, does it also suppress this supernatural energy?

Aside from its primary purpose of being *salt and light* to the world, the church was also called for the express purpose of nurturing and protecting the newly formed organism from heresy and exploitation from outside or imported sources.

The difficult questions to ask, and the difficult task needed, to separate the (often internal) diverging and conflicting issues are:

Can the *organism* exist in a safe balance with the *organization* that pretends to protect it?

Can the organization promote the organism's health and well-being without also promoting itself?

As said earlier, and it is well worth reviewing the point, *the Church of Power* (the *organization*), cannot produce the fruit of the Spirit anymore then the trellis can grow grapes. Only the *organism*, the vine of scriptures, can produce fruit.

It may not be overtly evident, but the world and the worldly are seeking for credible evidence of the Holy Spirit among and in us, the *Community of the Spirit*.

So, what is the true Biblical and appropriate evidence that this Spirit of truth is among us?

Why does our verbal communication not convince the world of our genuine purposes?

Is the world looking at the militant church to put into practice what they believe?

Galatians 6:22–26 provides us with a remarkable list of attributes of the new church which did not exist in the first century rabbinical law or religious establishment and is in short supply today:

Love	Joy
Peace	Goodness
Longsuffering	Kindness
Faithfulness	Crucified Passions and Desires
Gentleness	Self-control

This catalogue of attributes brings us very close to the very spirit of the militant church which arose on the day that the Holy Spirit baptized the awaiting believers.

The practical religious disciplines of Jesus day were a contrasting backdrop of intolerance and bigotry against the first century spirit of the new church. Historically a formalized religion has always attempted to shut down the free expression of the Spirit.

[5]Not that we are sufficient of ourselves to think of anything as *being* from ourselves, but our sufficiency is from God.

[6]who also made us sufficient as ministers of the new covenant, not of the letter but of the Spirit; for the letter kills, but the Spirit gives life.

2 Corinthians 3:5, 6:

Christianity, that is the spiritual energy as practiced in the first century, always brought with it a reprimand to the culturally degenerate philosophy and religion of the day. Historically, that has been the point of conflict between those who guarded their religious status and those seeking to rescue or reform the Biblical faith. The continued persecution of Christians, historically and in every case, is witness to the contrast which the first century *Community of the Spirit* demonstrated.

The features of the Acts 2 *Community of the Spirit* which we examine will be for purposes of comparison and to demonstrate how it is found now and to show that these early ventures have suffered quite a setback in our existing norms.

Acts 2:40–47 provides us the list of these features or the spontaneous values and practices for review and comment:

[40]And with many other words he [Peter] testified and exhorted them, saying, "Be saved from this perverse generation."

[41]Then those who gladly received his word were baptized; and that day about three thousand souls were added *to them*.

[42]And they continued steadfastly in the apostles' doctrine and fellowship, in the breaking of bread, and in prayers.

[43]Then fear came upon every soul, and many wonders and signs were done through the apostles.

[44]Now all who believed were together, and had all things in common,

[45]and sold their possessions and goods, and divided them among all, as anyone had need.

[46]So continuing daily with one accord in the temple, and breaking bread from house to house, they ate their food with gladness and simplicity of heart,

[47]praising God and having favor with all the people. And the Lord added to the church daily those who were being saved.

The catalogue of features in Acts 2, as they occurred on the first day after the coming of the Holy Spirit and through the subsequent years of struggle, is profound. The list is not a rearrangement of the Bible events, nor does this work try to demonstrate any ranking or necessary sequence or progression. Neither is there any interdependency suggested. Simply put, those activities all appeared and were all practiced then by the believers who were individually energized by the Holy Spirit.

In later years, efforts by churches to rate and practice these features of the early church have resulted in mixed outcomes and denominational divides.

Efforts were made by liberal churches to practice the apparent social issues at the expense of the teaching of the gospel truths, of prayer and signs and wonders, to a sinful world. The result was the liberal theology of the 19th century (1800s AD). Some have chosen to seek out the spectacular signs and wonders at the expense of the charitable issues raised by the actions of the early church.

The part can never be reckoned as the whole in God's economy. The model of the *Community of the Spirit* as shown in Acts 2 is simply the heart of God as displayed in the Word of God and played out by believers full of God's grace. There can never be a vital practice of Christianity that assumes a *cherry picker* mentality.

The Community of the Spirit Brings Positive Change

By and large, the work of charity which was resurrected by Christians in Britain about the time of the Industrial Revolution has been assumed by the State in many cases. We now seem to feel that we must go beyond our shores to do any meaningful charitable work. However, the beggar at the Temple gate is to be plainly seen on our streets and the injured "certain man or woman" (Luke 10:33) may live on our street. It is really not a case of *over there*, but all about us still.

We certainly are operating differently than the early church model demonstrated. We are not, now, living near that first century outpouring of Holy Spirit energy, as that church basked in the warmth of His love. The arrival of Christian values and overt love not only affected Britain's earlier need, but these same Christian values also rose up in indignation against all forms of slavery and oppression in America and around the world. The energized church of today still stands up to condemn the lack of care and concern for others in a world driven by self-interest and profit. It was reported that in 1988, North American churches assigned less than 2% of their annual income to "operate organized global Christianity."[13]

In 2001, only 1% of giving to missions went to unreached. For every $100,000 that Christians make, they gave $1 to the unreached.[14]

An online report[15] of Christian, North American activities show the following reported use of giving in North America in 2015:

- Pastoral Ministries of local churches, 96%
- Home Missions, 2.9%
- Giving to un-evangelized non-Christian world, .3%

James 1:27 says so clearly:

"Pure and undefiled religion before God and the Fathers is this: to visit orphans and widows in their trouble, *and* to keep oneself unspotted from the world."

Simple values and uncomplicated charitable actions of love are mandates which have been placed by God upon us all and have not yet been advanced or completed.

---

[13] George Otis Jr., *THE LAST OF THE GIANTS*, (A Chosen Book by Fleming H. Revell Publishers, Tarrytown, NY 10022, 1991), 237

[14] http://www.thetravelinglearn.org/stats/Mission Stats/The current state of the World/Status of Global Christianity

[15] As above

Perhaps the Christian society, so-called western church, has become overburdened by seemingly more immediate needs. Things demanding our attention and time; things like church attendance, budgets, staff wages, building plans, advertising programs, and other corporate church business. These have become our preferential programs of action.

There are so many modern issues that have been laid onto the burden of the Church as an institution. No doubt these issues are a result of internal pressures and external expectations. We find that, as a result, our corporate ambitions are not all that differently tooled out from those of the world we live in.

> *The world came knocking at the Church's door.*
> *He had a friendly face and we invited him in.*
> *We have become so accustomed to his presence here*
> *We hardly know how to invite him to leave.*
>> *John B. Duncan*

The successes and growth of the Community of Believers is a testament to the awesome intent of God to bring good into an evil world and to overpower the evil by this good.

By the year 400 AD, the Christian values inherent in the early church had eroded the pagan might of the mighty Roman Empire. The culture of oppression of its citizens, the low status of women and slaves, and its idolatry and superstition had weakened the pagan strength of the empire to a vulnerable state. Paganism just became unattractive and offered little to its adherents.

We must recall that at least half of the Roman Empire population was slaves and that female infanticide had decimated the availability of wives for the male population. As well, expensive wars had reduced the balance of the sexes to a serious degree, a real problem. The Roman government became unable to defend its cities from the Vandals and Goths. Roman conscripts were inadequate to maintain and defend their empire, and as a result, foreign soldiers were recruited to their ranks.

The practices of the early Church's values, as we found in Acts 2, were to be the strength which turned the tide of history. The apostle Paul said, "Overcome evil with good" (Romans 12:21), not "mount a bigger army."

It seems that these Christian values were attractive to the pagan population and caused many to leave their idols and follow Christ.

Paganism was, in the end, found to be ineffective, unimportant, of small scope, limited power to change anything, and expressed a moral ambiguity. It simply didn't matter.[16]

The Culture Changed by the Active *Community of the Spirit*; Christianity in its response to the populist need; by choosing its values properly and not just seizing an opportunity to apply its dogma, will always bring about change to the culture it meets with.

This has proven to be true repeatedly as Christians lifted up the charitable banner of Christian grace and truth.

Not only does the preaching of Christianity to a population lift many from the captivity of sin and despair, but men go on to establish societal institutions and endeavors that further lifts the level of society's living to new heights.

Missionary efforts around the world have brought profound change to the nations which were touched by the practice of the values of the early church.

Missionaries came to India as a result of efforts to go where the East India Company practiced trade. China was opened to the missionaries on the back of the war to allow the British to sell opium to the Chinese. Health care, education, and social reform followed everywhere the word of God was preached.

Countless examples are found throughout history of the benefits of the gospel being brought to pagan nations by the *Community of the Spirit*, empowered and sent by the Spirit. Christian men and women led the struggle against slavery, female suppression, and despotism of many stripes. They were seen opposing licentious lifestyles, built orphanages, etc., etc.

First Responders

The profound example of Acts 2 demonstrates a plan of the working of the Holy Spirit in any situation which requires change and improvement; not just the establishment of new moral codes, but the practice and application of resources to remedy obvious deficiencies in the human estate of the extant culture. This is true whether it is a work to revise a nation's moral core and fiber and its spiritual condition or a church which has floundered.

The *Appendix* of this work includes Worksheets for use (both Church-wide or personal) in listing and evaluating these principles.

---

[16] Rodney Stark, *CITIES OF GOD, The Real Story of How Christianity Became an Urban Movement and Conquered Rome*, (Harper Collins Publishers, New York, NY 10022, 2006)

1. Values

God's perspective on humanity is immediately displayed and quickly brought into practice as an antidote or an action to be taken to repair the condition. A mistake often made by well-meaning people is to apply the values which are primarily of a religious nature and overtly impose these as an antidote for the situation or problem in the culture. God's true values are always an improvement to any situation and provide a physical remedy for a society to move upward or forward.

By using the term "God's values," it does not mean that we retreat into a solitude or a cave to find solace from a perverted world system which has created problems. God's values, true values as demonstrated in Acts 2, spring from a heart that has been fixed on following and obeying Christ's teaching. God's values include the welfare and sanctity of human life.

The plight of the poor and disposed which the *Community of the Spirit* were awakened to, apparently had been offered no redeeming values or merit by the religious world of that day. Pagan religious or materialistic philosophies will never see any merit in improving the conditions of the poor. As Jesus replied to the Pharisees, "the poor you have with you always," He was echoing the requirement under the Law (Deuteronomy 15:4). "Care" carries a mandate of action, not merely an observation, or a feeling.

Only true Christianity seems capable of applying the values of explicit and concrete care for the needy.

So then, values such as mutual care for the health, feeding, warmth, and shelter from the elements were supplied to those needy people of Jerusalem. There does not appear to be any judgment upon the recipient's worthiness.

The resources for this charitable cause come not from the excess of supply, but from the believer's own storehouse. These values, and only a few are touched on here, were in sharp contrast to an overtly religious culture and later to pagan cultures.

In the Gospels, Jesus taught us a lot about God's values. This charitable work, which demonstrated new values, was a major cause of retaliation and pushback from the vested culture as the exercise of these values brought condemnation to the existing norms. People don't seem to like their customs disturbed by change, even when this change brings improvement to the outcomes in other's lives.

This teaching and practice of the Apostles, which contradicted the existing pagan or religious mythology, also brought a new sense of freedom and joy to its recipients. This freedom was realized in the sense of being set free from the endless efforts to improve the pagan worshippers and the religious people from futile religious practices.

Colossians 2:8 instructs us: "Beware lest anyone cheat you through philosophy and empty deceit, according to the tradition of men, according to the basic principles of the world, and not according to Christ."

The world is often offended by the simple truth and practice of the word of God. The teaching and the practice of inherent values and the whole list of 15 features shown in our Acts 2 model offends any culture principally because these values demonstrate how empty the espoused worldly values are.

2. Order

The Christians of the early church did not become compulsive, unthinking radicals as they began to manifest new values within their society. Order was soon developed by which they effectively brought these values into practice. Order was developed by which these values were demonstrated to be helpful. Order did not precede values, order followed as a response to effectively address the need. These values were not of a religious order nor a spiritual ranking of the worthiness of the recipients of charity. What happened then, of course, was the challenge of confronting how they should fulfill the mandate of the values brought about by the Spirit's prompting (a challenge that all good enterprises require). Whenever values are realized, then effective methods and means of ministry need to be established. Next, systems of distribution would have been instituted, all to serve the need of the poor more effectively.

Order did not overtake values, but order was established to serve the distribution of the results of their actions of charity to the needy. Order must always be the servant to values or order will soon establish its own set of values.

3. Structure

Structure is what the early Apostles were soon required to establish. The act of charity towards the poor widows who were of Hellenistic background was the value which they were responding to. In this case, a group dynamic was developed in response to the overload of responsibilities falling on the Apostles. This structure was established by agreement within the body as the apostles were released from "serving tables daily" in order that their time and efforts could serve other values of the established charitable practices. They were effectively reassigned to the task of preaching the Word, which was one of the adopted values.

This action was not the diminishing of the values of serving nor did this structural action, as it further developed into leadership assignments to the expanding church, overshadow the order or the values first developed.

We should examine our established church structures to ensure that these structures which we have developed or adopted are not the master of our ministry but the servant of the initial values of the *Community of the Spirit*.

We can easily adopt ranking of ministries and pigeonholes for appropriate actions to the degree that we easily end up serving the structure which was intended to become the servant of order and values.

The structure can have no meaningful value in itself unless the wisdom and utility of its expression is seen to assist and support the espoused values. Organizationally, the *Community of the Spirit* remained a very flat and responsive organism as the Word of God was preached and spread beyond Jerusalem and into the Gentile cities. There was initially no need or place for Archbishops or Cardinals because each church was autonomous but remained in fellowship with other churches with common cause. These churches practiced communication, not control.

Territorial authorities were not needed or established to safeguard any church ritual or dogma. The basic values which arose and energized the church were still the driving force. These early century Christians still functioned as a community of believers and were motivated by the leading of the Holy Spirit.

These dedicated men and women of God were not seeking self-aggrandizement or notoriety as they served the community where they lived. They were not vulnerable to heresy because they had already heard the authentic Word of God at the feet of the Apostles. Nothing of the gnostic or pagan doctrines was of any value in assisting them to move forward into the world. They had been and continued to be energized by the Holy Spirit.

4.   Cause

So many of the issues of our day (and the past) seem to be driven by an agitated, "generous acts," *cause* of some sort or another. Often, however, these causes degenerate from the original issues and become just a form or shadow of the first concern. The *cause* soon takes the pre-eminence and requires intermittent stoking of its fervor, but alone and without values to keep it on track, drifts into some unintended purpose. We soon are able to justify the loss of original values for the sake of the urgency of the cause. Ambition and reputation, on the personal or corporate level, takes the supremacy. Our values which started the action are soon diminished or lost to memory.

The working out of the "kingdom of God" which Jesus taught and demonstrated, was the original cause displayed at Pentecost; "but seek ye first the kingdom of God" (Matthew 6:33). The welfare of the kingdom and its progress and the care of its subjects was immediately seized upon because the kingdom of God was not seen as a *sometime, far away*, nor as a nebulous venture, as some seem to advocate today. Jesus taught that if He drove out demons from a person's life, then the kingdom of God has already come among the people of His time (Matthew 12:28).

It may be a hard stretch for us today to realize that, in God's eyes, the kingdom of God within a man or woman's heart is vitally more important than the welfare of any organization. Today, organizational goals and values are often weighed by the value of the organization rather than the value of the individuals who are a part of the organization and carry the passion to complete the establishment of these values.

The values which are foundational to the kingdom are soon compromised whenever the welfare of an organization or denomination takes precedence over the welfare of the organism and individual that it takes responsibility for.

Causes must be examined periodically to ensure that they serve and are subject to the welfare and values which gave rise to its platform.

Cause is to be the servant to the initial values, and must remain so, or we soon are found to be going astray. As well, our effectiveness is lowered to a status of idolatry of the organization at that point.

Diversity Serving a Common Purpose

Let me further comment on these four stated principles of the early church: values, order, structure, and cause.

We must understand that the character of the four principles mentioned will develop differently in various groups of people. They are, however, foundational to the various groups' experience in Christ and the pool of the need the group finds itself serving. This character will also be reflected in the ministerial aspirations and abilities that arise in the group.

We should not advocate a regimented program or methodology in coming to an understanding of the four principles. The features must be living and active, perhaps even subject to review and improvement as they are exercised. We must, under the direction of the Holy Spirit, develop the organism of our influence so that it can effectively carry out the responsibility for our calling which has been given to us.

It soon becomes apparent, as we press on in our walk of faith, that each expression of the *Community of the Spirit* will, of necessity, customize its activities to suit its calling, but never compromise the body of believer's true character demonstrated in their approach to fulfilling their own unique calling. Diversity is not the enemy of effective ministry.

Diversity which serves a common cause will always add its own dynamic strength. Whenever diversity is allowed to work into a cause, synergy is found to accelerate the effects of the work.

Whenever we fear diversity's dynamic strength and all its various abilities and talents, we very soon fall into a rigid formality and dogma void of creativity and the energy of the Holy Spirit. We very soon will begin to display liturgy and ritual to represent the original values and energy that the Holy Spirit gave us to witness to the resurrection power of Christ.

Aspiring to develop a framework of the four principles found above, one soon realizes they are not governed well or controlled by liturgical doctrine or creed. We do not approach the hungry, for example, from a doctrinal bias or a conditional methodology as we administer food aid. Jesus said, "Inasmuch as you have done it [feeding the poor] unto the least of these you have done it to Me" (Matthew 25:40). Just simply to draw out your resources for the benefit of the poor, that is what is required.

Unfortunately, the history of the church, both Roman and Protestant, has tended more towards paternalism; controlling the masses rather than ensuring they were nurtured and fed. The mid-1800s found many organizations going to the poor, wherever in the world they were found, and delivering aid in the same manner as the original Pentecostal church. Some still do but struggle with obtaining adequate resources from the believing church who still prefer to send rather than go as Jesus taught. The vast majority of Christians, for various reasons, are content or conditioned to sit in their comfortable pews and experience their weekly entertainment and fellowship without much regard for the poor and dispossessed which are referred to in Isaiah 58:6, 7:

> *6Is* this not the fast that I have chosen:
> To loose the bonds of wickedness,
> To undo the heavy burdens,
> To let the oppressed go free,
> And that you break every yoke?
> *7Is it* not to share your bread with the hungry,
> And that you bring to your house the poor who are cast out;
> When you see the naked that you cover him,
> And not hide yourself from your own flesh?

These are the same religious folk who criticized Jesus for sharing bread and fellowship with the poor and needy.

By His death and resurrection, Jesus taught the end of the Law. In doing so, He completely fulfilled the Law and gave us two laws by the new covenant to fulfill in the *Community of the Spirit*:

One, love God with all our soul, mind, and body and
Two, love one another as we love ourselves.

He did not offer rules, dogmas, or liturgy as a means of carrying out these laws, but He gave us a heart and a mission to do it always and wherever. These two commands must be paramount to all our ecclesiastical ambitions.

An introduction by example of better and more useful values always threatens, then weakens, the status quo as people adopt new standards of values. This is true whether the case is one of reforming a liturgical church or even a wicked and self-indulgent culture. Every successful missionary endeavor would indicate that such is the case. Jesus preached and demonstrated new values, not new rules. The values He taught were demonstrated, not merely idolized.

Liturgy portrays, but does not demonstrate, the truth of the gospel. Liturgy easily becomes tradition. This Church liturgy was owned by the Roman church leadership; it also soon became the practice of many Protestants. Standardized liturgy is often found to be an effective control mechanism for suppressing the expression of spiritual freedom in the unlearned masses.

In the hands of the ecclesiastical leadership, the *"works of God,"* as defined by the Church, were dispensed by the Church, the organization. This attitude towards the poor is not unlike the practice and attitude of the Pharisees of Jesus's time.

As ignorance decreased and the availability of the Bible prevailed, so faith changed from blind obedience to dogmas, to become a case of following the Word and the Spirit. Faith arose from the availability of truth, and the tradition and the presumed authority of the Church was thrown off by sincere folk who sought the freedom of faith that Christ provided. "Faith cometh by hearing the Word of God" (Romans 10:17).

Change, even outside of a religious framework, is resisted at first by those most affected. Our own comfort zone is not easily abandoned, even if it is wrongly located.

The Roman Church's liturgy and dogma was of their own making. It represented an amalgam of Old Testament rituals, Roman State practices, and pagan routines. It soon became standardized Church tradition. It was neither reflective of Jesus nor the *Community of the Spirit*.

~ PART FIVE ~

Reform and Conflict

The Reformation confronted the authority and the control which Roman tradition had placed on every facet of the lives of these European people of faith. It soon also controlled every facet of daily life, by decree.

The newfound faith of the Reformation was placed upon the Word of God. The maxim of that time became *"Sola Scriptura"*—"the Word of God alone." No private interpretations were allowed. Roman tradition was outrightly rejected.

However clean that break with the traditional Roman religion appeared to be, many of the taught principles of these traditions prevailed in giving scope and direction to the new Christian realities. Governance, ministry methods, practices; all came under evaluation against scriptural examples and teaching. This was contrary to the Roman Church's stance on their own traditional authority.

Real Ordained Authority

The balance of authority and the demonstration of that authority within the body of believers is to be found in the practice and degree of authority which the body has released to its head, Jesus Christ. Positional truths, such as that of righteousness and authority, require a practical *walking it out* to be effectively manifest in our lives. We cannot say we have authority when we are not under God's authority. Even Jesus said He was under God the Father's authority, "Not My will, but Thine be done" (Luke 22:42).

As the church body practices its spiritual submission to Jesus Christ, it will assume a greater collective, internal authority over external forces, issues, and conditions.

Our "power over all the power of the enemy" (Luke 10:19) cannot be realized in full faith force until we have completed our own presentation of a living sacrifice in faith to the Lord. The seat of Christian authority in the church is to be realized within the body of believers; the Community, not the Organization.

All authoritative positions within the body must receive their authority from the body, or the concept and exercise of authority is distorted. This is one reason that some churches chafe at their organization "placing" pastors over them, and others insist on the right to choose their own leaders.

A pastor, for example, receives his authority *in trust* to exercise his responsibilities within the body and his ministry from the body and not by ecclesiastical decision. Whenever a breach of trust occurs between the body and the pastor, there is an immediate loss of confidence within the body and a loss of authority on the part of the pastor.

The Donatists of North Africa in the years after Constantine rejected the authority of bishops who had submitted to Roman leaders and handed in scriptures to be burned by the State. They considered such leaders to have "lapsed" in their faith, and the Donatist Church of North Africa no longer accepted the authority of the lapsed leadership to teach and to perform church rituals. This was the cause of a major disruption of Rome's authority.

Aside from the civil authorities who exercise legal authority over the body's activities, as they affect the population, there are no legitimate, external authorities who can legitimately exercise spiritual authority over the body, the *Community of the Spirit*; Jesus is the head of the church, His body.

The early church, the subject of our interest, did not provide for a hierarchical spiritual authority over a local body of believers, precisely because Christ was the recognized head and the authority residing among those faithfully called to follow Him. The bishop (local overseer) or pastor that cared for and watched over the spiritual growth and welfare of each local body of believers was political in nature and arose out of ambition and carnal means of dealing with external issues. Again, this bishop/pastor received his authority from the body who selected him under the guidance of the Holy Spirit to serve them. There were no over-bishops in the early body of believers. What transpired between separate groups or communities as they arose in towns and cities was collaboration and communication, not submission to authority.

In later centuries, the Church of Rome sought to formalize the Church's newfound authority into a central entity which mirrored the ambition and structure of the Roman civil government. Remember that, until recent times, these newly minted churchmen were part of the Roman civil governance. In their attempts to exercise this centralized authority, they wrongly developed doctrines designed to subjugate and control its adherents. Personal faith in Christ as the means of salvation was supplanted for faith in the faith of the Church. Under their regime, the expression of personal faith in Christ had no merits. Salvation was to be held and dispensed by the clergy at an appropriate time of purgatorial punishment for sins; sins that Christ had already dealt with effectively by His death and resurrection.

Forgiveness of sins, a grace directly accessed by faith in Christ, was deemed the prerogative of the authoritarian Church and was taken away and reserved as a prerogative of the Church. It was these and many other introduced pagan practices (and many more traditions skewed from the Bible truths) that the Reformers rebelled against. Again, *Sola Scriptura* was these men's authority to act in faith for their lives, not Rome's distortional traditions and authority.

In another vein, some itinerant ministers active today seem to exercise "extra-church body" authority which is claimed to stem from special revelation or calling. However, these men or women, today, do not have an Old Testament mantel of prophetic authority. These itinerant ministries are raised up, recognized, and are to be supported, by the same *Community of Faith* who are to benefit from their ministries.

These modern-day prophets, evangelists and apostles will only be found to be exercising proper biblical authority, which the Lord has released to the body, when this authority is confidently and trustfully released by the body to these outside ministries. No itinerant or outside ministry can assume a higher authority which it might claim originates outside of the body of believers. This stance is just not Biblical, nor does it have a right to exercise its authority over the body or its selected bishop/pastor.

Authority must always assume a stance of ultimate responsibility which a "come and go" ministry never enters into.

The rightful position that externally connected ministries must maintain is that of a brother counsellor or advisor, never a fraudulent position of authority within the activities or ministry of the body.

Christian Authority

The modern Church has become a display of both meaningful and fanciful purposes. Some ministries exist as a platform for an ambitious leader who will use the church to achieve his own personal goals. Fame, fortune, and notoriety often proceed up the parade before a true and humble dedication to the Lord's calling. The demise of such leaders, by stroke of God's hand or newly placed revelation, soon causes the demise of the weak supporting church.

As for the fanciful ends, some leaders have thrown off the good examples of scripture and sought to re-invent the church. Often, the label of "cultural relativism" is given as the new banner to march under. However, the culture of any society since Christ has never been a friend of the church. In order for a culture to be redeemed, it must bend to the teaching of Christ, but the church must never lose its authenticity; it's salt and light.

The real question that arises from these compromising activities is: are Church leaders who seek after personal fame and fortune practicing a form of idolatry under a new cover and a new definition? And whenever we go about building a church on other than the Solid Rock Jesus, is this not also a form of idolatry? Or when we seek to build up a political arm of the church under the guise of establishing the kingdom of God on earth, are we not forgetting Christ's directive, "The kingdom of God does not come by observation" (Luke 17:20)? Verse 21 further identifies this kingdom, "For indeed the kingdom of God is within you."

The Roman Church of Constantine's time made a grievous error, largely driven by the ambitions of the sons of Roman nobility as they stampeded into the newly approved and funded "Christian" Church. This Roman Church, filled as it was by ambitious, non-regenerate sons of Roman nobility, brought with them the desire to re-energize the Roman seat of power in a time of waning empirical fortunes.

Bishoprics were bought and sold by the ecclesia after Constantine gave the nod to the Christian Church. Distant cities had the office of bishop established and sold to the highest bidder. Many of these bishops never or seldom left Rome to serve in the bishop office in cities away from Rome, yet collected 25% of revenue from these distant churches. Pagan practices and celebrations were instituted as a means of assuming the pagan population under the guise of Christian tradition. This perverse Christianity, infiltrated with pagan doctrines and carnal behavior of the clergy, soon polluted the Roman Church in such a fashion that it caused many righteous and pious Christians to leave the stench of the ecclesiastic realms of Rome and to set up semi-autonomous monasteries. These monasteries generally served the public better by setting up schools away from the influence of large cities. These schools were a venture directed to improve the lot of the peasant stock who were also taught the gospel message. In the process of teaching the gospel, they were educated in many practical disciplines of learning.

These monasteries also taught better farming and animal husbandry and provided a market rationale to these people as a means of marketing their excess produce. In doing so, they introduced the fledging form of fundamental capitalism.

This study of God's creation soon led to the beginnings of science as they overcame ignorance and superstition, but this bonus was only realized when they left Rome and its religious, political corruption.

The early Celtic church, which began as a mission soon after Constantine's nod of approval, brought a charitable and uplifting tone to the Irish people of these early centuries. The work of land improvement and infrastructure, as well as farming methods, soon began to relieve the burden of poverty. Education lifted the masses from ignorance and bred into the Irish mind a love for prose and poetry. This work continued and was expanded into some parts of Western Europe until this movement was almost destroyed by the Viking hordes. The Irish missionaries fulfilled the mandate of Acts 2 and turned their efforts to converting these Vikings in their own homeland.

These monks and missionaries, wherever they went in France and Germany, demonstrated James 1:27:

Pure and undefiled religion before God and the Father is this; to visit orphans and widows in their troubles and to keep oneself unspotted from the world.

The monastic movement continued their work of charity demonstrating the spirit of Acts 2 until they were overtaken by the Roman ecclesiastical directives.

The modern Protestant Church is not unspotted, as they so easily set aside the charitable and missionary actions which have changed the face of the global cultures in need of the redemptive work of Christ. The effect of the church's original mandate is not easily seen in the internal church structures. Perhaps it can best be seen in orphanages and hospices, leprosy missions, addiction recovery centers, and other ventures which show mercy and compassion; but even more so, the *Community of the Spirit*'s work can be witnessed in the loving care in these places. It can also be readily seen as Christian men and women move pagan cultures away from superstition and cruel practices by these 15 features of Acts 2.

The Trellis and the Vine

All too soon, the fruits of early Christian evangelism were overlaid with the implementation of stiff doctrinal practices and narrow behavioral patterns. Too soon, the church efforts moved from "the truth shall make you free" (John 8:32) and "he whom the Son sets free shall be free indeed" (John 8:36) to a condemnation of religious leaders of Jesus day; "for they bind heavy burdens, hard to bear, and lay *them* on men's shoulders, but they *themselves* will not move them with one of their fingers" (Matthew 23:4).

The overtly imposed religious doctrines and practices which followed sound evangelistic efforts weighed down the minds and hearts of men seeking truth and freedom. The truth that sets men free is so readily subjugated to deadly binding religiosity.

Religious leaders who have some measure of success in primary ventures are too often attracted to the work of setting up the political arm of the kingdom of God. This has always been a tempting pitfall, but never Christ's mandate.

Under the pretext of establishing the earthly, political kingdom of God, the ecclesia soon set up rules and practices to constrict the freedom of the laity. The ecclesia changed their focus from Christ as their source to the Roman church as the authorized dispenser of God's grace and freedom. This "new" style of freedom can be seen as an imposed measure of practice to be achieved by compliance to rules of order and behavior. Faith in Christ and a personal relationship to Christ is pushed back by this regime as of less importance, and the verities of this spiritual authority is touted as the only way that it can be realized through compliance to the new imposed order. That is a classic way that cults operate. However, denominationalism is not immune to his tactic either.

There is always a battle to be fought and won against this insidiously imposed order, as men and women of integrity take the Bible teaching truth and overthrow the oppression of the imposed religion. They undertake to re-establish the original premises of Christianity through their exercise of personal faith in Christ's work of redemption and salvation.

Early in the Reformation, and perhaps as a necessary tool of the Reformation, the printing press was invented and the Bible was printed in the vernacular languages. This was followed by sincere seekers of God re-directing their allegiance to Rome's imposed pagan authoritative religious system of control and oppression. This retraction of allegiance was followed by Rome's persecution and punishment of the retractors.

As it was in Rome, so it is wherever people of faith reject the hierarchy of the ecclesiastical system imposed on them.

But let's return to an earlier statement: "the grape trellis does not exist except for the sole purpose of supporting the vine." The trellis of our ecclesiastical construct, even if much decorated, is not capable of producing the fruit of the Spirit of the Bible's teaching. An imbalance of wicked proportions exists whenever the welfare of the vine is subjugated for the benefit of the trellis. The purpose of the Church, the organization, is meant only to serve and support the mission of the organism; that is, the *Community of the Spirit*.

Approving the Things that Are Excellent

And this I pray, that your love may abound still more and more in knowledge and all discernment, that you may approve the things that are excellent, that you may be sincere and without offense till the day of Christ (Philippians 1:9, 10).

The alabaster jar, or flask, of the Bible was celebrated not only for its own beauty, but was always understood to be a vessel which was set apart to contain a substance which was very special or even precious. It was not a jar of clay which was used to hold common everyday commodities.

Perhaps an analogy could be drawn from this example to describe the church and its commodity, the organism, the *Community of the Spirit*. The Church, the organization, is not the treasure to be admired, albeit unique and special. The treasure that we can discover is to be found within the alabaster jar. It is this commodity of the *Community of the Spirit*; unique, precious, and rare, the treasure in the alabaster jar. The treasure is not the alabaster jar.

As we further examine the early church's success and the many meaningful revivals of faith through the centuries which followed, we see four essential and fundamental characteristics that ensured their success:

1. It may seem obvious to say so, but Christ must be glorified in all that we do. The Bible teaches that it is true. It is easy to become caught up with promoting causes and personalities to the point that our primary goal of glorifying Christ is overshadowed by causes and people. Christ must be glorified or else the light and purpose of our endeavors are diminished by lesser causes. I Peter 4:11 states, "…in all things God may be glorified through Jesus Christ, to whom belong the glory and dominion forever and ever. Amen."

2. All efforts made on behalf of the *Community of the Spirit* in these actions were to serve the common good. The benefactors of the early church were those who received the charitable gifts provided by the believers. God himself, who blessed and sanctioned this good work, caused growth and increase. There seems to be no apportioning of benefits towards or promotion of the donors.

3. The work and outcomes of the Holy Spirit among us is not for private blessing or consumption. Just as Jesus said that He "did not come to be served but to serve" (Matthew 20:28), so we ought to seek out opportunity to pour out into other lives what is poured into ours. Jeremiah 48:11 declares a just principle by which to govern ourselves: "Moab has been at ease from his youth; He has settled on his dregs,

and has not been emptied from vessel to vessel. Nor has he gone into captivity. Therefore his taste remained in him, and his scent has not changed." This is a simple commentary of how self-interest causes our Christianity to become stale and offensive to those who thirst for the water of life.

4. All believers are meant to function spiritually. The Bible clearly instructs us that we are all called with purpose and meaning. To live a life that denies God's claim on our lives, that is, to not function like this truth declares must be lived out in our daily lives, is perhaps the single most offensive act that we can commit against Christ and the body of believers. A lost world requires our light and salt witness and the body requires our participation. We may have been threatened by the unseen ghosts of the world's system, or we may have been made to feel ineffective and insignificant in our capacity to shine as lights or as the flavor of salt and its preservative quality. Regardless of how we have been threatened, the mandate of Christ to serve others still stands.

And we know that all things work together for good to those who love God, to those who are the called according to *His* purpose (Romans 8:28).

However, Jesus *bothered* to ensure that men have recorded His comments about these little issues. Matthew 10:42 mentions the reward that is to be received by faithful ones who put themselves out when they "give a cup of water in His Name"; and again in Matthew 25:40: "assuredly, I say to you, inasmuch as you did *it* to one of the least of these My brethren, you did *it* to Me."

What we all need to understand is that when we all participate in the grand plan of redemption, personally and actively, we provide a measure (however insignificant we might think it is that we do) that the Lord can multiply for His purposes. Consider the mustard seed of His teaching and how it grows to become a great tree (Matthew 13:31). We all need to put some seed in the ground, personally.

Just like the Samaritan, we need to take a risk with our reputation and make a habit of getting our hands dirty while engaging the work of the Lord. Subjectivity in Christianity is often not a bad thing, but objectiveness will turn us cold and formalize our response to the needs of the world. The decision is ours to make. Jesus, you may remember, got involved with the unattractive people who simply needed love and charity. The religious elite mocked Him for His actions. They who would someday experience the great gnashing of their teeth and the pain of hell as He judges them on that great day.

Mostly, our biases and prohibitions are of our own making and have been developed for our own protection because of perceived contamination from the world we live in. We desperately need to venture outside of these self-imposed limits, into the marketplace of human struggle in order to effectively preach Christ's redemptive plan for mankind.

Can you imagine what your church would look like and act like today were we to take the original model of Acts 2 and transpose it into our time and our place in the world where we each live?

What should we do about the established overburden of ecclesiastical form, ritual, doctrine, and religiosity that prevails today in church activity? Is this something that can be corrected and implemented in one fell swoop? Is there a quick fix for the dilemma that we are accustomed to seeing today?

Most quick fixes soon fall apart and necessitate either a continuous fix or change. We do have a roadmap to more sound practice of Christianity which will fit into any age. A re-occurring remedy is found again in the adoption of the Acts 2 Model. But it necessitates a change of focus from ourselves to others in need of the gospel and charity.

The Lord often allows painful affliction and even outright persecution to disturb the tranquility of the church in repose. Such persecution of the western church would necessitate a re-invention of our present church model. It would require a change of great proportions if the church was to survive as did the church in Russia, China, and several other countries in the not too distant past. The church in these countries experienced religious persecution but prevailed and grew by sharing their light and salt without the help of the superstructure of an established church.

Meeting Opposition

For those today who rest upon a sense of privilege and entitlement as a credible Christian witness to the world, change is abhorrent. Our worldly successes are often portrayed as a fair demonstration of God's approval of our practices. To these people, success is seen to be evidenced by church attendance, staffing of professionals, wages, budgets, notoriety, and fame. The early church could not boast of these features, but it certainly did turn the establishment upside down. The Church is no longer seen as a threat to the world's wicked system, but we are certainly threatened by it.

Just remember that the Roman Church, after Constantine's captivity, began to get rich from state funding, and every effort was made to use this approval of a Roman dictator to justify their actions of the heretical expansion that followed. The inherent pagan values of the waning Roman Empire also soon found its way into the expansive actions of the Roman Church. Such a Church would have surely looked and acted differently if the pre-Constantine persecution and oppression had continued into the centuries that followed. The outright inclusion of pagan cults as new peoples were conquered by the empire was probably viewed as a creditable means of expansion for the Roman Church. The Roman Church simply captured the pagan countries by encapsulating their religion, rebranding it, and subjugating the expectations of the people who had been taken captive.

From a time of great social strife, Dostoevsky wrote several books which subtly criticized both the Russian state and the corrupt State Church. The retribution that followed indicated that Dostoevsky had struck a sensitive issue in their clamor for glory.

In his book *The Brothers Karamazov*, a work of fiction but a definite exposition of the church of his times, he writes a section called "The Grand Inquisitor."[17] In it, he provides great insight of the ambitions of the church in his day. Perhaps this work of fiction was just too close to the truth to be discounted by the authorities.

He writes in this chapter of a fictional time when Jesus temporarily returns to earth at the time of the Inquisition of the 16th century. As this chapter begins, we find the Cardinal freshly returning to the town from his recent foray of burning several heretics who apparently threatened the serenity of the church's composure. He finds Jesus performing a miracle of raising a young girl from the dead on the steps of the cathedral as the funeral progresses. The people recognize Him and flock to Him in adoration. The Cardinal has Jesus arrested and jailed for His interference in the things religious. He accuses Jesus, "Why then art Thou come to hinder us? … All has been given by Thee to the Pope…and all therefore is in the Pope's hands, and there is no need for Thee to come at all. Thou must not meddle for the time at least."

Further, the Cardinal argues, "Didst Thou not often say that, 'I will make you free' … For fifteen centuries the people have been wrestling with Thy freedom. Yet they have brought Thy freedom to us. But let me tell Thee that now, today, people are more persuaded than ever that they have perfect freedom, yet they have brought their freedom to us and laid it humbly at our feet." He claims it as a merit for Himself and his church that, at last, they have vanquished freedom of faith and have done so to make men happy.

---

[17] Fyodor Dostoevsky, *THE BROTHERS KARAMAZOV, the Constance Garnett Translation revised by Ralph E. Matlaw*, (W.W. Norton & Company, Inc., 500 Fifth Avenue, N.Y. 10110, 1976) 227–245.

Again, later he states, "We have corrected Thy work and have founded it upon miracle, mystery, and authority."

This chapter, "The Grand Inquisitor," is a worthy read for us today. We see that Christ's freedom brought with it a sense of conscience which is hard for us to bear unless we act upon it in a Bible way.

Roman, Greek, Protestant churches of various stripes, and all Christian faiths have traded some of their freedom of faith and its attending conscience for the constancy of ritual and dogma. And in doing so, have established "miracle, mystery, and authority" to reinforce the same.

We have so readily taken Christ's assigned responsibility for a lost and dying world's welfare and have become, to too great a degree, spectators, and admirers of those who assume ecclesiastical authority over us.

The potential for change by our present church is profound. Many of our modern churches have become centers for the worship of human idols and for passive observation. We too have traded the freedom of faith for "miracle, mystery, and authority."

With few exceptions, we do not begin to outdo the church of Pentecost; rudimentary, albeit effective, as it was. Salt and light we may be today, but in minute degrees. We seem quite content, for the most part, to hide our light under the gilded bushel of organized religion as we tend our personal pews. Or perhaps this gilded bushel is of our own philosophical machinations of pretense and fear. As stated previously, we desperately need to venture outside of our self-imposed limits into the marketplace of lost souls, and to be found there, faithfully preaching Christ's redemption to a lost world.

~ PART SIX ~

The Roadmap to Revival

This commentary in examining the *Community of the Spirit*, which was energized at its onset by the Holy Spirit as He intruded into the religious mindset of its day, is not complete. Some sense of recapturing this energy and finding a suitable application for today's worshippers will be required as we progress. Criticizing what this original organism has transitioned into would not be complete until it offers a redress to its waywardness. In the pages to follow, we will attempt to roadmap a change to better ways of serving Christ and the world in which we find ourselves.

In the western world, many Church organizations have become like large corporations that employ scores of dedicated people who serve tirelessly to achieve the stated vision of the organization they find themselves functioning in. They are encumbered with goals, budgets, programs, hierarchy, real estate care, and maintenance, and many more temporal issues attached to the work of faith. Meanwhile, we are looking over our shoulder, so to speak, for the world's approval. We offer little to applaud except, perhaps, management of our ministries towards secular, approved organizational goals.

For many of these organizations, declaring a stated purpose gives direction for the organizational efforts. It is quite in vogue in church circles today to produce Vision Statements. In fact, this "vision casting" in itself has become a significant consulting business. Often, these Vision Statements are merely "want to be" statements, or they may be the statement of the corporate ambition. In some cases, the statement reveals a desire to compete and become an entity to be admired and attractive to others.

In many cases, the Vision Statement only vaguely addresses or recognizes the legitimacy of Christ's claim for the church and His directives. In these cases, the attractiveness of the Acts 2 church has been diminished as being not culturally relative to the forces at work in the world today.

Some Guidelines Apply to Vision Casting for Churches

As Church organizations and individuals begin to examine their assumed or hypothetical vision affirmations, they must evaluate their assumptions. The following statements may serve as points of consideration in the process of their deliberations:

Vision is about **becoming,** more than about **achieving** desirable ends.

Vision cannot be imported successfully but must be generated from within the organization. The inherent energy and stimulus of the Holy Spirit must be understood and annunciated. A local church carries its own history of beginnings, successes, and even failures. Its "purpose" is even stamped in its "DNA" and represents its unique "call."

Vision's success in a church setting is mostly subjective but can be objectively regarded. It should, however, avoid objective goals. After all, Jesus said that "the kingdom of Heaven does not come by observation" (Luke 17:20).

Vision is not corporate ambition clothed in ecclesiastical garments.

Vision must be supported by the values, processes, and the structure of the Organization in order to bring the Vision into reality. Fervent activity gets us *spinning*, but not building up the *Community of the Spirit*.

Vision is subject to evaluation periodically. A living vision will recognize errors, successes, and new opportunities for effective service.

Vision is to be practiced, not merely revered.

Church organizations which appear to have succeeded according to the worldly standards of today often are a poor representation of the heart of the first church, the church of Pentecost's day. The same ambitions that motivated the Roman Church are clearly reflected in our present forms of seeking for credibility and success. The world that fights the efforts of the church of our roots cannot be assumed to be a creditable judge of kingdom values.

Luke 6:46 holds a rebuke for those who set out to fashion a church in their own image: "But why do you call me Lord, Lord, and do not the things which I say?"

Frank Sinatra captivated the music world with his recording of the famous song, *I Did It My Way.*[18] This song seems to capture the spirit of the times. We so quickly adopt the attitudes of the world into our church practices, but as Romans 1:22 states, "Professing to be wise, they became fools."

How close to the rebuke of Matthew 7:22, 23 do we choose to stray with our own choices?

---

[18] Paul Anka, *I Did It My Way.* 1969, Composer and Writer

[22]Many will say to Me in that day, "Lord, Lord have we not prophesied in your name, cast out demons in your name, and done many wonders in your name?"

[23]And I will declare to them "I never knew you, depart from Me you who practice lawlessness."

These questions then can be credibly raised:

Can you really be an authentic church practicing first century values in an anti-church society?

Must we be like the world in order to be judged by them as acceptable?

Can today's church survive without big budgets and impressive assets?

Is Christianity identifiable without the trappings and rules of our churches today?

Are the accoutrements of our religiosity necessary for our authenticity?

We must be reminded, from time to time, that Jesus said, "I will build my church" (Matthew 16:18), and that God still has His place in its conduct. "For the time has come for judgment to begin at the house of God" (1 Peter 4:17), and if it begins with us first, what will be the end of those who do not obey the gospel of God?

1 Peter 2:4, 5 also sets our course plainly:

[4]Coming to Him *as to* a living stone, rejected indeed by men, but chosen by God *and* precious,

[5]You also, as living stones, are being built up a spiritual house, a holy priesthood, to offer up spiritual sacrifices acceptable to God through Jesus Christ.

And again, we are admonished;

… I *write* so that you may know how you ought to conduct yourself in the house of God, which is the church of the living God, the pillar and ground of the truth (1 Timothy 3:15).

The Kingdom of God

Is this to be taken as an abstract term or did Jesus refer to a concrete concept? Did He refer to a physical realm to be observable through the ages or a metaphysical kingdom, a visionary concept to be idolized but not realized until He returns in His day of triumph? Did He refer to our Christian organizations designed primarily to serve His cause by way of its lands and temples of worship attended by its varied devotees?

Now, when He was asked by the Pharisees when the kingdom of God would come, He answered them and said, "The kingdom of God does not come with observation…" (Luke 17:20).

What did He refer to when He said that "the kingdom of God does not come with observation"? Does this statement conflict with Revelation 1:7 where it is stated, "Behold, He is coming with clouds and every eye will see Him…"?

Do our religious concepts require a concrete observable presentation in order for us to arrive at a settled faith in His words? Perhaps, as a widespread understanding, the eye of faith is missing in our dogmas.

Over the centuries, men of religion have stumbled over Christ's presentation and over Him as its reigning and present Sovereign. Religious men have variously gone about setting up physical and observable representations of the spiritual concepts and precepts of the elements of the Kingdom of God.

However, the Lord has the last word in this matter as Acts 7:48 declares:

However, the Most High does not dwell in temples made with hands…

Contrast that statement with 2 Corinthians 6:16,

… For you are the temple of the living God. As God has said:

"I will dwell in them
And walk among them.
I will be their God, And they shall be My people."

Great structures, like the Basilica of Rome and many others in history, both Roman and Protestant, have been erected and embellished so as to represent the glory and presence of God. Many organizations and doctrinal frameworks have been contrived to represent His glorious and manifest presence, all done even though scripture declares He does not dwell within the constructs of man. For the most part, these attempts at representations, whether in stone or words, have become idols or phantoms of our imagination.

[20]Now, when He was asked by the Pharisees when the kingdom of God would come, He answered them and said, "The kingdom of God does not come with observation;

[21]nor will they say, 'See here!' or 'See there!' For indeed, the kingdom of God is within you" (Luke 17:20, 21).

When Christ spoke of the kingdom of God being within us (Luke 17:21), did He purposely leave us without a legitimate description of the kingdom of God? Is this kingdom within us some resident power or, perhaps, some admirable virtue? Can it (the kingdom) or does it, rule and reign? How does that happen, and how do we know when this "kingdom" is present or active?

Jesus once said:

"For where two or three are gathered together in My name, I am there in the midst of them" (Matthew 18:20).

We, today, however, seem unaffected until we see the hundreds or thousands together, rather than accepting that the significance of the two or three will realize the presence of Christ. The scripture, "the kingdom of God is within you" (Luke 17:21), provides a perspective on the spiritual or internalization of His presence rather than the observable.

On one of the many occasions when Christ was opposed in His ministry, He replied:

"But if I cast out demons with the finger of God, surely the kingdom of God has come upon you" (Luke 11:20).

Here, He is openly declaring to the unbelieving Pharisees His position as the king of His kingdom. He is implying that where the kingdom was manifest, there the king was present in His kingdom.

In this case, He was speaking of the kingdom of God and definitely not the anticipated return of David's kingdom.

So then, the logical conclusion we may arrive at, is that the kingdom of God is manifestly present wherever Jesus the King is. That case is now true only when the Holy Spirit, who speaks for and represents Jesus to this world, is active on behalf of our faith.

No church or physical edifice can truly represent the kingdom of God, even when we set up altars, or thrones, or seats of authority for His earthly selected representatives to sit on or to exercise their earthly authority.

The megalomania of every age requires that edifices and memorials of a visual and objective nature be erected in order to annunciate its greatness and to guide and control the collective followers.

Jesus pointedly did not demonstrate or resort to such activities which easily became idols of remembrance. As Hubert Newton (1830–1896) said, "Christ founded neither a church nor a state. He handed over no laws, nor a government, nor any form of external authority; but He tried to write the law of God in the hearts of men in order that they may govern themselves."

Also, He left no prophetic direction as to these actions evolving into a Church institutional framework for the years to come.

As the saying goes, "The heart is the heart of the matter."

Once Philip, who would later be known as Philip the Evangelist, asked of Jesus, "Lord, show us the Father, and it is sufficient for us" (John 14:8). This petition, which begs of understanding, was not unlike the scribes and Pharisees's demand:

[38]"Teacher, we want to see a sign from You."

[39]But He answered and said to them, "An evil and adulterous generation seeks after a sign, and no sign will be given to it except the sign of the prophet Jonah" (Matthew 12:38, 39).

The fact that Jesus refused to demonstrate a visual representation of the invisible God and directed the apostles' interest, the manifestation of the Spirit in men's lives and hearts indicates that the unseen heart issues were the considerations to take away from the Lord's manifest presence.

The kingdom of God, the unseen vital parts of our lives, indeed, is where God chooses to rule and reign. As noted, "the kingdom of God does not come with observation" (Luke 17:20). This excites in us a desire to know God by His works and His manifest presence.

How readily we fall down to a lesser resemblance of His presence by physical representations that excite the eye (or ear) rather than His kingdom of the heart. Where the King is, is His kingdom. Where He is, no other can take up authority and rulership.

We most readily exercise our believer's authority against our enemy's works and invasion of territory when we make room for, and activate our faith in, His sovereignty and presence. Two kings cannot inhabit the same position of power, the same throne. Where Christ reigns, the devil cannot. However, just by being physically present, we do not threaten the devil's reign; we must exercise our faith and Christ-given authority by allowing Christ to reign in that moment in our hearts. A work of faith, which must be a discipline, is evident in our walk of faith on any day, every day.

In other words, the faith action works by a daily submission of our lives to Christ and by walking out our obedience.

Obedience to Christ is not just the total content of our "do it" guide. We have been given the "go ye" activation by Christ which propels us into the world's realm of sin and disobedience, an activation which demonstrates His presence and power.

Jesus must have dumbfounded His detractors and followers when He stated, "My kingdom is not of this world" (John 18:36). The political pressure of the times, as Israel lived under Roman oppression, demanded a current prevailing ruler to overthrow the physical and mental oppression which the Jews of that day suffered under.

So, this statement, "not of this world," caused many to turn their support away from following Him.

In fact, today our population suffers from the same conflict. Can a kingdom "not of this world" and which does not "come by observation" satisfy the spiritual and emotional inclinations of those who seek His lordship? And how do the secular people of our day assimilate this teaching?

The demonstrations and trappings of present religion proffer some comfort to the seeker and resolve to those who are confused by the many voices calling out today. However, in the end, do these religious expressions supply us with what Christ was intending as He spoke out the following words?

[28]"Come to Me, all *you* who labor and are heavy laden, and I will give you rest.

[29]Take My yoke upon you and learn of Me, for I am gentle and lowly in heart, and you will find rest for your souls.

[30]For My yoke *is* easy and My burden is light" (Matthew 11:28–30).

Perhaps the more important question is: does what Christ offered to His followers satisfy the spiritual hunger and longings of the sincere seeker? Do we even comprehend what Christ offers or are we too distracted by the attraction of the objective manifestations of our present religious practices to grasp His meaning?

Historically, men and women of conscience have left the lights and noise of society and retreated to solitude of various kinds in order to find Christ's presence and meaning. Sometimes they have retreated from the world to the point that they have entered secluded caves to find Christ's presence.

We find ourselves, so often, thinking about out proper place both in God's kingdom and in the world we are born into. Is it where we are allocated in our various institutional functions or as the Spirit of God designates? How often we seek permission to be just who we are in Christ? How do we balance the various demands and pressures of our various stations in life?

What does Christ offer us for clarity?

He says, "Go into all the world…" (Mark 15:16).

Paul says, "Do not be conformed to this world…" (Romans 12:2).

John says, "…as He is, so are we in this world" (I John 4:17b).

"As He is in the world"? Do we not reckon Him to be in heaven? How is He here in this world?

For some people, it is quite a spiritual stretch to know that Christ is in heaven making intercession before God's throne (Ephesians 1:20, Hebrews 7:25), and at the same time, He is here with us in some realized representation or state. Yet He said, "I will not leave you orphans [comfortless], I will come to you" (John 14:18). Here, He was speaking also of the coming of the Holy Spirit.

The Holy Spirit, as you may realize from reading John 16:13–15, has no mission or purpose of His own but to "guide [us] into all truth and to glorify Christ." He is also to "take of what is mine [Christ's] and declare it to you."

So we cannot readily separate the purpose and presence of the Holy Spirit from Christ's purpose, except that Christ completed His earthly purpose, and the Holy Spirit brings and declares that Christ's declaration of truth is reality. His purpose in the world is one of declaration and reconciliation, and we are the instruments He has chosen for this task.

It is so vitally important to the purity of His cause of reconciliation that we do not compromise His purposes with our earthly ambitions to the extent that we realize that His kingdom, which "does not come with observation" and is to be realized "within you" or "in your midst," can strive to maintain His spiritual intents.

Clearly, the Bible declares that He does not dwell in places, and perhaps we need to include forms and traditions of our own making.

Acts 7:48–50 declare His position on our presumptive craftiness.

[48]However, the Most High does not dwell in temples made with hands, as the prophet says:

[49] *"Heaven is My throne,*
And earth is My footstool.
What house will you build for Me? says the LORD,
Or what is the place of My rest?
[50] *Has My hand not made all these things?"*

Isaiah 2:5 furthers this topic of discussion:
Their land is also full of idols;
They worship the work of their own hands,
That which their own fingers have made.

Whether we bow down to our own representative works to worship, or our larger edifices of veneration, we do avoid the strategic realization that these are not the accoutrements of godly worship but simple distractions from our Godly purposes.

Stately edifices of worship adorned with trappings of wealth are motivated just as David's ambition to build God a permanent house and demonstrate our carnal approach to the kingdom of God. Man's selection of opulence does not truly reflect God's glory among us. Yes, we are impressed and even awed by these representations, but the New Covenant is not of, or in, the flesh, but of the Spirit; specifically, His Spirit in us who are transformed to His attributes and character, and by these activated attributes as they shine out into a dark world of sin.

~~~~

How do we demonstrate these heart issues?

Our motivation is from the Holy Spirit demonstrating that the kingdom of God overcomes the kingdom of darkness.

Do we go about building concrete depictions (idols) of spiritual things?

Is the "among us" characteristic, of the Holy Spirit, not displayed by character and the fruit of the Spirit?

~~~~

Whereas the Old Testament method of overcoming opposition rested on the skillful application of the sword, the New Covenant has taken the sword away from our arsenal.

The covenant of the Spirit provided by Christ and written in His blood has brought us into a spiritual confrontation with evil. Zechariah 4:6 foreshadows this action, this change of tactics:

"Not by might nor by power, but by My Spirit,"

Says the LORD of hosts.

Many respected prophets in the Christian church today warn us of a time soon upon us, a time of subtle persecution and overt oppression emerging from an unfriendly attitude against the church; which originates with the State. Many political leaders who espouse a one-world government view the various expressions of Christianity as divisive, regarding their promotion of a one-world secular humanistic culture as the only acceptable goal for mankind.

The noted evangelist and author offered this statement (which might jar our sensibilities):

The chief danger of the church today is that it is trying to get on the same side as the world instead of turning the world upside down.[19]

Turning the wicked world upside down was what the early church was accused of by its detractors (Acts 17:6). We seem to be incapable of this holy task, so we hide our light under "gilded bushels." Then we seem to delight in drawing attention to our gilded bushels.

The first church, as an entity, was a work of the Holy Spirit. However, we find in Acts 2 that it was at odds with the spirit of the culture it found itself in. The church is called to promote and display the kingdom of God at work. The world system promotes itself and will be judged and destroyed by Jesus, the Righteous Judge who sits on the throne of God. The world has intently labored to proscribe the church's works of righteousness and its proclamation of the

---

[19] George Otis Jr., THE LAST OF THE GIANTS, (A Chosen Book by Fleming H. Revell Publishers, Tarrytown, NY 10022, 1991), 237

work of God. This preaching of the kingdom's values of righteousness raises a voice extant culture. How then can the church find a place of cultural relevance which some Christian leaders promote today? Culture seeks its own fame, glory, and fortune. Culture is not a good soulmate to the ventures of this *Community of the Spirit* of God.

James 4:4 succinctly says it all;

Do you not know that friendship with the world is enmity with God? Whoever, therefore, wants to be a friend of the world makes himself an enemy of God.

In speaking of the coming of the Holy Spirit, John 16:8–11 says:

[8]"And when He has come, He will convict the world of sin, and of righteousness, and of judgment:

[9]of sin, because they do not believe in Me;

[10]of righteousness, because I go to My Father and you see Me no more;

[11]of judgment, because the ruler of this world is judged." [Jesus teaching]

Some scriptures do not leave us with a lot of options but cut very close to where it begins to cause reflection and even pain. It is better to be corrected than to be judged.

The big question remains then; is what we call the Christian church of our day an honest or creditable reflection of how this church of the Day of Pentecost began to combat the world's systems? Is the rich church of Laodicea, portrayed in the Book of Revelation, really a reflection of the rich western church of today?

[17]"Because you say, I am rich, have become wealthy, and have need of nothing—and do not know that you are wretched, miserable, poor, blind, and naked—

[18]I counsel you to buy from Me gold refined in the fire, that you may be rich; and white garments, that you may be clothed, *that* the shame of your nakedness may not be revealed; and anoint your eyes with eye salve, that you may see"(Revelation 3:17,18).

The Laodicea church appears to have had trouble clearly seeing itself for what it was. Do we, too, play mirage games with the truth? How important has the applause of the world become to us? Or how important has a favorable review of our "church" by the culture become? Do we listen intently enough for the voice of the Lord saying, "Well done, thou good and faithful servant"?

At this late date in church history, we must soberly reflect on some pertinent facts:

1. The Church is still Christ's domain, not ours.
2. He provided a profoundly effective model of values and practices when the Holy Spirit came to a crowd of His believers.
3. The model, in so many ways, has been re-manifested through history as God revived peoples and nations by the preached word of God.
4. Signs and wonders, as we have seen portrayed in the Bible, often were the companions of preaching as God "confirmed the Word."

~ PART SEVEN ~

To the Glory of God

Therefore, whether you eat or drink, or whatever you do, do all to the glory of God (1 Corinthians 10:31).

[26]"Yet it shall not be so among you; but whoever desires to become great among you, let him be your servant.

[27]And whoever desires to be first among you, let him be your slave—

[28]just as the Son of Man did not come to be served, but to serve, and to give His life a ransom for many" (Matthew 20:26,27).

How readily we mix the water with the wine; the leaven of the Pharisees with the flour. Our real dilemma is that we often justify or even sanctify such poor behavior and ask or expect God to bless it.

These fraudulent practices are neither sanctified nor are they blessed by God, and we can't seem to find a way out of our systematic muddle.

The gilding of the bushel seems to be more important than the light it overshadows. So we continue to modify and polish the gilded bushel, and the lost world is still very, very lost.

When will the church begin to achieve the blessing which was so apparent in our studies of the infant church? It will be evident when ecclesiastical authorities begin to seriously divest themselves of their interest in their own glory and fame in the eyes of other men of faith.

A credible conversion of practices and values must begin if we are to see the idle pew tenders begin to assume their own God-assigned role of local light bearers. These light bearers, in action, are truly the strength of the *Community of the Spirit*.

An intentional divesting of interests of lesser corporate values must also be undertaken by the leadership. In most cases, this cannot be considered a light or quick task to be accomplished. Often it is a painful process which may be misunderstood by the leader's peers.

The affirmation of leaders and value provided by their relationships within the ecclesiastical system they serve will be directly challenged by this divesting action. The "well done thou good and faithful servant" (Matthew 25:21) approval must be preserved as a blessing of the Lord and valued above any earthly accolade.

This re-evaluation and statement of values is primarily a heart issue which Jesus was so careful to teach, Matthew 5, 6, 7; The Sermon on the Mount, which could be called the Constitution of the Kingdom. When we get the heart issues right, we will find that the external issues are easier to deal with. Remember that the kingdom of God, which we pray "will come," is about internal issues, not external. People have been stumbling over the difference of heart and external virtues (perception and reality) for centuries. We have often been seen building cathedrals and churches instead of building up lost lives.

Church growth—honest, healthy growth—comes when the *Community of the Spirit* gets it right.

And the Lord added to the church daily those who were being saved (Acts 2:47).

Success, if that is the correct word (perhaps fulfillment is a better one), comes as the church assumes and lifts up regained standards or values and disseminates them into the world.

Allocation of resources, including those for suitable facilities, is vitally important in order to undertake the tasks which now begin to come to light as these values are established in the organization.

Any outright changes must be owned and managed by the leadership. Changes, not merely resetting of old values or repurposing of old wineskins, must be the means of advancing towards the work of the Lord. Don't carry the past futile practices into the future and expect new results.

People are often offended or confused by change that is not understood. When the elimination of old, tried, and true values are concerned, this is more so. Sacred cows are not easily abandoned. Wisdom in adopting new values, and the proper annunciation of them, is profoundly an important task to be undertaken by the leadership.

Often these changes of values begin with an examination of the spiritual history of the individual church; that is, what has God directed and blessed in the past. This, in itself, is not easy, as these old tenets may have woven themselves into the tradition of the organization without due regard for their genesis. It is not simply a case of removing the old ideals and replacing them with trendy new methods of ministry. The values are the heart of the matter, not just a new style.

The eradication of the props of tradition that have supported a redundant, ineffective religious system is necessary as the new values are implemented. These new values, as taken from Acts 2 of our study, must be customized by its patrons in every case to suit the various church plants. The practice of these values will, of necessity, be expressed somewhat differently in every church as the real dynamics of the Holy Spirit begin to establish and bless compliance to the Spirit of the new covenant practices. It is easy to fall into a legalism of values and practices and should be avoided. A certain dynamic of ongoing change determines if an action is alive or dead.

No copycat work here will survive. Such actions only create idols to be revered and looked back at. They have no ongoing redemption of time and effort. The expression of values cannot be imported from other organizations—do your own heavy lifting and struggling for authentic expressions. The heavy lifting and struggling to give birth to authentic values cannot be done by a surrogate body, congregation, or leadership.

The New Testament is charged with meaningful directives by which we enrich our Christian lives. Whether we reference the Sermon on the Mount, Christ's teaching of not judging sinners, or the many lessons to be learned from the Epistles of Paul, they all serve us as well. It would seem that our present corporate church values in today's ministry often eclipse, or outrightly ignore, these espoused sacred Biblical directives. It is very sad to find that the forces which detract us from serving these Biblical values have soon redefined our mission. Our concern soon is found to be serving these new values, not those demonstrated by the early church.

We seem to hope that someone else in the pews is attending to these vital issues. These sacred directives are not often annunciated and promoted into our planning and execution. Too often, they are the tag end of our efforts rather than the drivers of the establishment of our values.

Most of what Christ taught the disciples contained a moral imperative which should be part of our practice. Christ never intended that these tenets of obedience and faith should become idolized or ritualized, but that they should be overtly practiced by His followers.

"If you abide in Me, and My words abide in you, you will ask what you desire, and it shall be done for you" (John 15:7).

When these early church values become the practices of today's church, we can expect that if the pure Word of God is taught, that He will confirm these words with "signs and wonders" as Acts 2 highlights.

In many ministries, "signs and wonders" seem to have become a sideshow. Signs and wonders of a spectacular nature seem to be the goal of ministry instead of the fuller practice of the early church's ministry. There is no doubt that true signs and wonders turn the hearts of sinful men and women to God. That, of course, is their intended purpose. But the practicing of these original principles is as weighty a witness. They will still be evident when the sideshow is over.

If God is to confirm the Word with signs following (Mark 16:20), then the Word preached ought to be that of God's Bible; not the traditions, not the philosophies, and not the pet doctrines of men.

To the Real Task

All of the foregoing comments and discoveries are an objective evaluation of religious practices that have become normalized and reinforced through dogma, liturgy, and doctrine. These statements are necessarily negative if we are to gain any wisdom from studying these religious icons. The positive aspects of a vital Christian faith are easily extracted from Acts 2, the fifteen features outlined there, and from the re-occurring revival outcomes which historically bring out the genuine faith characteristics.

Competition, ambition, and a search for perceived, cultural power or relevance in a secular world have seduced the minds of the people who have lost their sense of Christian values. We so easily venerate worldly notables and admired values in our culture and soon adopt them for use in our own Christian creeds and practices.

A recent case in point seen to be playing out in some areas of doctrine is that issue which deals with prosperity. Several years ago, many investors in the financial market went wild with greed and began to perilously leverage their assets in pursuit of ever-increasing profits. This action by the investors was pursued as an American right to get rich and prosper.

Almost in lock step, it seems that some undisciplined, and perhaps even greedy, Christian leaders seem to be taken with the notion that having worldly riches is an appropriate expression of Christian faith. This pursuit was followed by marginalizing many sound and proven Biblical values because the blessing of riches became primary. These newfound riches were seen as a sign of God's approval and blessing of faith. This action was esteemed while the poor of the world were largely un-evangelized and unaffected nor benefitting by this richness. And we once more gilded the bushel.

This venture was gilded with several scriptures which were appropriated from the intended purpose of truth, and then getting rich became the intended goal. This getting rich took on some perverse expressions, and these newly blessed rich were applauded with adulation from their followers. Adopted carnal cultural values did not do the *Community of the Spirit* any favor but diminished the true charitable character of the church.

So, is this Laodicea model of Revelation 3, or the Acts 2 Model, the correct Christian model to be followed? For many people, the big question is: does it really matter as long as you are happy? (By the way, "happiness" is the whole point of modern psychology and counseling.) Perhaps a better question to be asked is, which of the models, the Laodicea or the Acts 2 church, pass muster before the judgment seat of Christ?

Does Matthew 25:45, 46 make any significant meaning in this conflict?

[45]"Then He will answer them, saying, 'Assuredly, I say to you, inasmuch as you <u>did not</u> do *it* to one of the least of these, you <u>did not</u> do *it* to Me.' (emphasis by author)

[46]And these will go away into everlasting punishment, but the righteous into eternal life."

Does what we choose to do, instead of being obedient to the truth, carry with it any eternal consequences?

Does sincerity trump obedience?

Do we accept the values which Christ demonstrated and commended to our keeping?

Or does Psalm 106:15 point out the results of such perverted desires:

"And He gave them their request,

But sent leanness into their soul."

It begs the question then, doesn't it; whose church is it, His or ours? Can we blamelessly fashion the Church after our own image and our own culturally adopted values?

Many churches today have opted for the development of political influence and psychological persuasion as a means of advancing their particular interests in the kingdom of God. The original power of the gospel seems to have been offered a backseat to modern intellectual wisdom.

Jesus showed us how there is a distinct separation of His kingdom and Caesars (Luke 20:25):

And He said to them, "Render therefore to Caesar the things that are Caesar's, and to God the things that are God's."

Our efforts at building a kingdom of God by political means is not what Christ had in mind. The Roman Church of the early centuries showed us how that type of venture goes awry. God seems to be always correcting our errant ways.

Well-founded Christian leadership is about:
- the teaching and the practice of Biblical truths;
- the work of instilling these truths into the hearts and minds of those who sincerely seek to follow God's purpose for their lives.

  It must also:

- help to impart strengthening spiritual experiences in order to bring about changes to people's lives and behavior and
- empower people towards a victorious witness.

As people are empowered, they should be encouraged to find their place of spiritual vigor in the work of the gospel of Jesus Christ. The Holy Spirit is, in fact, active in these same tasks by way of exalting Christ. Politics and the art of perception is all about humanism, a very deadly foe of Christian values. Humanism is just old Greek philosophy dressed up in a three-piece suit of today's respectability.

There is a vitally important lesson of values which we repeatedly need to take a renewed interest in. Namely, it is that of seeking first the kingdom of God. Let God take care of the addition of things and perceptions.

This is not simply a diatribe against the many worldly values that we, as a church, embrace; it is, in fact, the words out of Jesus's mouth.

We regrettably value the opinion of the politically correct world above what we will be ultimately judged for before the judgment seat of Christ:

For we must all appear before the judgment seat of Christ, that each one may receive the things done in the body, according to what he has done, whether good or bad (2 Corinthians 5:10).

It should be noted that the axiom of "political correctness," which is so current in our conversation today, was a maxim developed by the communists after the Russian revolution as a means of controlling dissent. A very oppressive tool of controlling the population. Political correctness should not be part of our modern Christian conversation or interest. It is really just censorship cleverly disguised as current wisdom.

~ PART EIGHT ~

Mission Conflict

Two serious questions to be asked are:

Must western churches abandon all that the years of planning and labor have produced in building what has become a respectable demonstration of Christianity to society?

Can the leadership of our denominations simply walk away from their religious establishments as the *Community of the Spirit* begins to demonstrate a new Bible vision for the church?

The churches of the established society of today must do something that is both significant and notable if they are to be sustainable and be recognizable as God's *Community of the Spirit*.

If persecution by the State takes the form of removing the charitable status of the church that spends a significant portion of its income on self-perpetuation and maintenance, wherever expenditures on the works of charity are considered to be minimal, how then does this kind of church justify and continue to survive?

If the preaching against sin, perversion, and disobedience to God's laws from God's own word, the Bible, becomes classified as hatemongering, how does this Church endure? In many instances, this action has already begun by the State. Preaching has been classified as proselytizing, and censorship against the church is issued even though there are yet no laws to restrict preaching. Some segments of society have already classified preaching the truth of the Bible as hatemongering.

If criminal charges are laid against the proponents of Christianity because the Church's moral virtues differ from those of the State, what then? Where, then, in society, does the Church, under such duress, find creditability and favor? Some countries already practice such overt discrimination against Christians today.

Some pundits tell us that this regressive action has already been undertaken by the State. Our pet doctrines and programs may be under fire when they differ from the State's moral imperatives. When all that we value as a church organization is taken away, we may be left with something that is a weak shadow of the early Acts 2 church.

The secular humanistic State has begun to establish itself as the moral standard of society. This reactive action has robbed the Church of its moral and spiritual high ground. Soon the Church will be left with the imperative to preach the State's moral code or face the consequences. That's what happened to the Orthodox Church in Russia.

Merely strengthening our present established position may provide us with more of what we have already, not that "something else" that we require to be effective witnesses of our Lord's approval and blessing.

It is only when we assume the role of the Acts 2 church that we demonstrate that our gospel is superior to the State mandate of morality.

Those fifteen values (see pages 38 and 45–62 in this work) found in the early church may have to become our point of salvation in our time. Redemption will come to the gutted church as we empower and practice the original values and practices. As the church gives credible witness of the Acts 2 profile, we will bear credible fruit before God to a lost society.

Usurped Leadership

Over time, centuries in fact, the ecclesiastical opportunists of Constantine's era of history assumed the establishment positions of authority in the Church. They also appropriated the exclusive right to the sacred practices of the Church. This action set the clerical hierarchy in exactly the same position as the priests of the pagan temples who exercised their various cultic regimes. Gradually, the population was reduced to a spectator status and lost their ability and right to function in the Church in any Biblical and meaningful way. This pagan practice was established within the realm of the Church, and its governance became a mirror of the Roman civil regime. Instead of Senators who elected Caesar, the Cardinals performed that function to elect their Pope. No longer did the lay people elect or choose their bishop as in historical, early Bible times, and the subjugation was soon complete.

Honorable and sincere men and women were kept ignorant and silent under this authority. The Church took no role in teaching and training the masses of their population. Not unlike *The Grand Inquisitor's* statement of "miracle, mystery, and authority" (see pages 71, 123, 124) instead of the freedom of faith which Christ provided us with as an effective means of serving Christ.

The ecclesia favored and protected their newly wrought positions of authority and power so much that they began to persecute, torture, and burn those who opposed their newly assumed authority.

This practice of professional practitioners and their exclusive rights to authority is found in some measure in many Churches other than the Roman style, and they teach this facet of leadership to the lost. The case is sometimes made where only the pastor has the final authority to interpret scripture. The scripture, however, assigns the position of truth teacher to the Holy Spirit on a personal basis. John 14:26 and 1 John 2:27 reference the Holy Spirit and the abiding anointing as the source of truth:

"... But the Helper, the Holy Spirit, whom the Father will send in My name, He will teach you all things, and bring to your remembrance all things that I said to you" (John 14:26).

But the anointing which you have received from Him abides in you, and you do not need that anyone teach you; but as the same anointing teaches you concerning all things, and is true, and is not a lie, and just as it has taught you, you will abide in Him (I John 2:27).

That is not to establish religious anarchy, but to enshrine the freedom of faith.

So today, we may be found paying our dues to the professional ministers who assume our, the pew tenders, ministerial charges of "going and preaching the Word."

In our own several ways, we have severely neglected our personal charge and find our spiritual urges fulfilled by becoming interested but, largely, unengaged spectators.

Herein lies the vulnerability of the newly persecuted church. We are easily and complacently deceived and truly are not individually assuming a Christian, Acts 2, stance in our churches, marketplaces, and wherever we encounter the darkness of the world system. Our spiritual and emotional stance of compliance with the secularly established norms make us vulnerable to humanistic control and censorship.

Shining Our Lights

It is often wrongly assumed that the people of the pews are not dedicated, motivated, or sincere enough to stand up and let the light of the gospel shine into the marketplace. They are, though, quite capable of getting on with it. And they are, after all, the only ones who are found daily in the marketplace.

However, there is an imposed or assumed mindset which the community must deal with, because of many established forms and practices of Christianity which, frankly, just simply get in the way. It is often assumed that these lay people cannot be trusted or are inadequately trained to be entrusted with any significant ministry. Shining their light, that is their personal testimony of grace, is seen by many as insignificant or even improper ministry. Many are made to feel untrusted and incapable and begin to feel a certain reluctance to launch out into the depth of ministry to the world. Remember, the world shakers of the 1st century, for the most part, were just everyday people who had been touched by the Holy Spirit. Being discouraged from stepping out in a ministry of sharing their testimony of faith, often, is seen as lack of interest in their mission of faith, or even mistrust. We can attend a lot of advertised seminars about confidence building which deal with our feelings of inadequacy and still not get the point Christ made about our bushels, however gilded, which hide the light.

2 Corinthians offers a comment about the everyday Christian's usefulness and worthiness for the work of spreading the gospel (chapter 3, verse 6), …who also made us sufficient as minsters of the new covenant, not of the letter, but of the Spirit; for the letter kills, but the Spirit gives life.

It is by the Spirit who abides in each of us that this light is brightened to shine into the dark places of the world.

I Timothy 1:8, 9 informs us that we each have a task of salt and light witnessing to fulfill in our lives:

[8]Therefore do not be ashamed of the testimony of our Lord…according to the power of God

[9]who has saved us and called *us* with a holy calling, not according to our works, but according to His own purpose and grace which was given to us in Christ Jesus before time began.

~ PART NINE ~

The 15 Notable Features of the New Community of Acts 2 for Leaders

So, let us return to the Fifteen Features of Acts 2, the original model of the church, to discover how leaders in the church can influence a change of structure and purpose.

We all want to be found serving Jesus intentionally with our abilities and opportunities and our resources.

But to be intentional in our service, we may require a roadmap or a plan to follow.

From a leadership point of view and responsibility:

How are these fifteen features manifested in our churches?

How do these features compare with your stated purpose and your organization's vision and purpose?

How can these features be constructed and appropriated into your corporate values and your church activities?

There is both a leadership responsibility to recover an authentic Biblical estate to the things which pertain to the *Community of the Spirit*, and also, the membership of *the Community* must actively take their responsibility to be energetic salt and light as seriously as if this body of believers were presently standing before Christ's judgment. We must examine the leadership role first and then suggest a remedial role for all participants of the *Community of the Spirit*.

1. Enthusiasm

It is surprising how often the morbidity of church services and worship of Christ is also a reflection of the mood of the clergy. We are not lost now, and we are more blessed. God's intention is not to punish us for our past sins. The service to Christ should not be seen as a sore bed of suffering and pain. Such attitudes expressed in our Christian church are a carryover from past legalistic doctrines and liturgy. The lack of enthusiasm certainly is not a Christian virtue which was experienced by first century believers. It is profoundly important that an attitude of joy and celebration in our walk of faith is fully and sincerely portrayed from the platform of leadership. The disciples mourned at the death of Christ; however, they rejoiced at the resurrection. We live on the resurrection side of history, receiving that perspective; we should rejoice with those who were glad at the coming of the Holy Spirit.

Enthusiasm is a contagious commodity, and so is emotional stupidity. We must find a realistic balance by which we undergird all our work for the Lord. Primarily, the leadership's attitude, behavior, and communication is the heart of the matter. The heart of leaders should not be grave, but joyous. It may seem that a congregation of mourners is more easily led than a jubilant army of faithful followers of Christ, but mourners hang around dead matters, not living issues. Perhaps Christian leaders need to seek a new baptism of enthusiasm from the Lord.

2. Baptism

Baptism, as we see detailed in scripture, was a serious compact on the part of the new believer. As all things became new, there was a serious expectation of acceptance and fellowship expressed by the new believer who was leaving a life of sin and the religious culture of their time. He was, in fact, joining his life and future hope to the *Community of the Spirit*.

On the part of the church and leadership, it is of vital importance that significant long-lasting spiritual nurturing and growth opportunities are provided to the new believer coming to Baptism. Leaving the newly baptized to their own devices too often results in a return to their old lifestyles and habits. Without initial nurturing, the newly baptized often fail to grow in grace and the knowledge of the Lord.

This compact of baptism should make provision for a bond, a two-way agreement between the candidate and the *Community of the Spirit* and its leadership for the spiritual welfare of the baptismal candidate.

Every meaningful effort should be put forward by the body and the leadership to ensure that, by example and instruction, a full integration process will continue towards functional maturity. Baptism is one of the two Christian ordinances of faith that visually demonstrate a testament of agreement and acceptance. Marriage, also a coming together, is the other one found in practice in most Christian churches. It, too, requires the nurture of the body of believers.

Church programs should reflect an acceptance of, and responsibility for, new members in the *Community of the Spirit*. This is how a salient group becomes a *Community of the Spirit*.

3. Coming Together

The Community must demonstrate unity of function and purpose. It is fundamental that coming together is essential for the continued growth and the stability of the church. To ignore rifts and factions will only delay the manifestation of problems that will erode this community spirit; that is not to say that coming together is a work of conformity.

We can, each of us, conform to Christ's image and purpose in our lives and still display the all-important aspect of our personal diversity. Our diverse expressions, not our contrary nature, will be seen as a display of our faith and is communicated to the body for enrichment.

It takes a wise leader to understand and work with diversity in the body. Conformity to the cause of Christ can exist alongside the expression of diversity and personality. These two, conformity and diversity, are not necessarily mutually exclusive.

A much weaker organization operates with the idea of rigid or extreme conformity. Diversity is not an enemy of community but stimulates and enriches the expression of faith.

Cult devotion is measured by personal submission to a proscribed standard. Conformity to that standard is seen as the measure of personal belief.

Conformity deals with the annunciation of a common purpose or cause of the active body. Diversity is how that end is pursued. Conformity and diversity of expression easily support each other as they "come together." Wise leadership makes it so in their area of influence.

4. Teaching

In this case, teaching refers to the Apostle's doctrine (or teaching) of the gospel of grace. It is said that much of what is put forth as church teaching today is just so much rehashed humanistic philosophy. The so-called wisdom of man has often been found to usurp the pure teaching of Jesus and His Apostles in our church communities.

One of the struggles which the early church had to deal with was that many converts to Christianity had been educated in Greek philosophy. That education was used as a filter through which Christian teaching was viewed, e.g. Philo (20 BC–40 AD), a converted Christian from the Hellenistic Jewish tradition of Greek philosophy. This philosophy was man-centered, not God-centered, and is with us today as a pervasive screen.

The tools for teaching made available to leaders and teachers should necessarily be of the Spirit and not of some humanistic counseling, methodological sort. Colossians 2:8 raises the alarm in such human practices:

Beware lest anyone cheat you through philosophy and empty deceit, according to the tradition of men, according to the basic principles of the world, and not according to Christ.

The danger in adopting a counseling, psychological, humanistic framework that addresses wrong thinking or negligent attitudes is this: God honors His own Word, which, properly set forth, will address spiritual errors and issues.

Modern psychology and humanistic counseling address the results of wrong thinking and behavior and attitudes instead of the roots of sin.

We should be required to ask ourselves at some point, in a time of suppression or persecution, does psychology meet the need or are spiritual values the thing that wins the day? Do we so easily lay aside the teaching of the Hebrews 11:3:

"By faith we understand that the worlds were framed by the word of God, so that the things which are seen were not made of things which are visible."

The word of God is our sufficiency in all matters of life. Liberal theology teaches us that the word of God is not sufficient to our time.

Our teaching necessarily must be of the Apostle's Biblical-grade, produced in love as the fruit of the Spirit is active in our churches.

God's word, properly preached, produces God's witness even to the point of signs and wonders.

This effort of right, Godly teaching must be a result of a revival of proper values; values made real and experienced in our own moments of devotion to the Lord Jesus. At every opportunity, we need to avoid wasting time and effort whereby we chose to spread humanism's obtuse interpretation of the gospel in favor of sharing the Apostle's pure teaching. This action of preaching the full gospel is an intentional act, so, too, is the intentional act of deleting philosophy and humanistic values from our programs.

5. Fellowship

This word, *fellowship,* which has been translated here from Bible references, implies participation, not merely enjoying the company of others over food and drink. We often try to make our *together* times more meaningful by including food, drink, and perhaps entertainment. We do this as a means of fostering a spirit of goodwill and inclusion.

However, in the truer sense of participation, fellowship is about being personally involved in the church ministries; that is, all ministries. There cannot be made a case to rightly exclude the membership from every aspect of church ministry, especially as we apply the Acts 2 model.

Perhaps this *no-participation* action is what diminishes the volunteer roster in real ministry issues when help is needed in vital areas. A negative impression towards general inclusiveness is projected when we only applaud and include the *"stars."*

We are not the Roman Church and the distance between the professional and non-professional operatives in ministry is largely an illusion of the Church's own making. We are all called to God's purpose; we are all able ministers of the Spirit of the New Testament:

⁵Not that we are sufficient of ourselves to think of anything as *being* from ourselves, but our sufficiency *is* from God,

⁶who also made us sufficient as ministers of the new covenant, not of the letter but of the Spirit; for the letter kills, but the Spirit gives life (2 Corinthians 3:5, 6).

As leaders in the church, we understand from our references in Acts 2, the ministry must be shared by all as God in His wisdom leads and provides. It is the *"us and them"* exclusion that breeds distrust in the body of believers. This action blunts our faith by marginalizing our inspirational participation. This sense also directly paralyzes the effective witness of the whole body.

When the Holy Spirit was given to the believers on the Day of Pentecost, the outpouring was a lavish, without measure, action by God. This same Holy Spirit is still to be found among the believers of today and is actively growing the witness of the church as we give place by removing our doctrinal and denominational barriers.

The task of modern leaders is to bring release from imposed bonds of demonstration and doctrine and to encourage participation in the whole ministry by the whole body such as the early church did to great success.

Such action, that is, delegating and releasing ministry, would be seen by some leaders as leaving their charge of responsibility for the welfare of the body. It may seem to be a risk of unknown outcomes but, in fact, the body is edified through its own participation.

Body edification, of course, is a more meaningful and direct mission for leaders to pursue.

"But he who prophesies speaks edification and exhortation and comfort to men" (1 Corinthians 14:3).

A wise leader will forget about losing control; instead, will lead wisely. Don't quit your responsibility, but share it among faithful men and women in the body. It will require a new type of leadership and management to carry out pastoral prudence and training. The burden of leadership needs to be shared within the *Community of the Spirit*, making the burden lighter to bear.

6. Sharing of Food

Christian leadership cannot easily take the responsibility of sharing their personal larder of food with everyone who is in need. But perhaps this issue is greater than the supply of their own food. As leaders, it is possible to set up and implement church activities which encourage the whole church to share their supply. This can be done not just by sharing their excess food with each other but to the benefit of those who are found on the margins of the church membership. Christian charity carries a powerful witness to the lost.

However, sympathetic sharing of food should prompt dialogue and witness and an opportunity to show a salt and light ministry to those with whom we are sharing. It is hard to win the confidence of people when we minister with a cold approach to dialogue. We must show ourselves to be open and charitable in order to gain a hearing for the gospel we carry. Sharing the gospel can effectively begin with the sharing of our store of food.

It is sharing of food we are discussing here, not giving of financial means to buy food for the hungry who never will see the inside of your church or the light in your eyes.

Church people, as well, are often living in their own pockets of despair and worry. There are often very lonely people in church. Sharing food, real sharing, is an opportunity to minister to our own body needs. We need to do this for the health of the body.

Leadership can set up the venues, instruct people on sharing their hearts, and fulfill the obligations of "give and it shall be given unto you" (Luke 6:38).

We may excel at vicarious giving and delegating our deeds of charity; however, personal sharing, real one-to-one sharing of food and interaction with dialogue, will cause the true light and salt to be seen and understood by those we seek to bless. It also provides a personal opening and blessing to our lives. We are personally strengthened in our confidence as we learn to share from our storehouse.

Give, but always engage.

7. Sharing of Possessions

This feature of the infant church is not an easy tenet to describe and to promote in a materialistic society. Especially, it is the case where some churches seem to hold doctrines indicating that our possessions are a sign of God's approval of our Christian faith. Or, in other words, if you have faith, get your own stuff.

Paul the Apostle counted the loss of all of his things "as dung compared to the glory of Christ" (Philippians 3:8). We're not there yet. We can readily give away our excess, but not so easily our treasure.

Churches must come to the place of surrendering their things by clear demonstration to the unsaved that possessions, prosperity, facility, goods, and their own resources are available for sharing with all who demonstrate real need.

Remember the good Samaritan (Luke 10:30–37) who felt no obligation religiously to help the man who had been beaten and robbed. What the caring Samaritan did shamed the charity of the religious elite. (Please see the poem *Passing by on the Other Side*, in the Appendix.)

This personal sharing of possessions provides the opportunity to develop a personal relationship with the needy. It also demonstrates that we acknowledge God as our own source of provision. There is no religious decree that keeps us back from personally giving to the need of others. Our prejudice will provide us with that excuse, just as the Pharisees tried to criticize Jesus for personally showing charity to the unwashed of His day.

It will never be enough for us to preach the cause of sharing or to develop any slick charitable response to needs when we do not personally demonstrate the same first century spirit of charity in our lives. Leaders can change people's perspective on possessions by proper teaching.

8. Agreement (Concord)

Disruptive disputes in church activity must always be observed as an indication that the devil is making inroads. He will use the fleshly desires of members over miserly and paltry issues to disrupt the flow of charity which the Holy Spirit desires to be the lifeblood of our church. Christ's blood is the lifeblood of the church.

Most disagreements have historically occurred over minor issues. Therefore, it is vital that the leadership not become embroiled and distracted by these lesser causes and identify them as such.

If the church ministry is not pursuing large, vital, or major ministry themes, then minor things become a distraction significant enough to tax our resources. Sometimes, personal ambition and petty politics area at the root of such disruptions. These must be dealt with by the leadership, and those who raise issues that disrupt the concord of the body must be corrected in order to see that concord will be blessed but disagreement never will be.

It is presumed that the Church has already established its own values, order, structure, and cause, and is actively going about fulfilling this end. When these features become mere slogans, distractions will inevitably occur.

The communication of these values and features of the New Testament church to the body of believers is essential. The practice of fully applying the

Church's resources to achieve its desired goals is essential because it demonstrates that there is no internal disagreement over values.

We all definitely need the Holy Spirit's wisdom and abiding presence to continue a sense of agreement. Peace, or concord, is the outcome and will go a long way towards showing the light of the gospel to a lost world. It will also untangle any confusion over the proper application of our personal abilities, interest, and resources.

9. Gladness and Simplicity

There is nothing that occurs in church activities which will dull the interest and participation of believers more than morbidity and complexity. The pagans and heretical sects load their religion with ritual, dogma, liturgy, and conditions that must be performed by attendees in order to gain the approval of their gods.

It was Jesus who said, "for My yoke *is* easy and My burden is light" (Mathew 11:30), and it was Jesus who condemned the Pharisees and Sadducees "for they bind heavy burdens, hard to bear, and lay *them* on men's shoulders; but they *themselves* will not move them with one of their fingers" (Matthew 23:4).

Jesus set the tone for our continual service to Him and to the body. In John 8:36, He declared, "If the Son makes you free, you shall be free indeed."

It was this freedom of faith, which the legalists of Jesus's and Paul's day hated so much. They extended their clerical powers to silence these ambassadors of the faith by killing them or punishing them.

As leaders, we must guard against teaching by example, or word, anything which will diminish the effect of this freedom which Christ provided. People who come to Christ already carry their own baggage and we must go out of our way to ensure we don't add to their emotional and spiritual loads. We are instructed to offer the freedom which faith offers us, the release from bondage.

Some Christian leaders assume that a good load of fear, shame, and quilt will keep new believers from returning to sin. However, those who continue to carry a load of sin and shame and don't experience the release of repentance. These people soon realize that their faith has no admirable or contagious freedoms to share.

People, lost or saved, seek after the freedom which Christ alone can provide for them. Leaders need to teach and demonstrate this freedom of faith. The freedom of faith is found among people of gladness and simplicity. The gospel is quite simple, and it needs to be seen and practiced as such.

Simple faith is easily defended from attack and criticism from outside.

10. Praising God

It is evident in scripture that the praise of the people of God is a vital part of their relationship with Him. Every recorded victory of the Old Testament saints was accompanied by exuberant praise.

Praise is where God chooses to manifest His glory;

"But You *are* holy, enthroned in the praises of Israel" (Psalm 22:3).

Praise is never shown in scripture symbolically by ritual, dogmas, or tradition, but praise is to be vocalized and demonstrated.

Praise is not to be observed as a spectator event; that is, the stage performers sing, play, and otherwise entertain while the pew-tenders observe. That is not an adequate demonstration of Godly praise. Of course, praise is more than music, but it has been said that music is the language of the soul. What better way than song for the redeemed, regenerated soul to express praise?

Church meetings should always engage the congregation in praise worthy of the God they purport to serve.

It is the personal expression of praise that changes the dull expressions of religion into vibrant and victorious Christianity. Mainly, praise asserts victory and releases faith as God inhabits this praise.

Praise should not be considered as a distraction to our church service. It will be the main event at some future date, a heavenly celebration, as we, the believers, gather around the throne of God.

Christian leaders who realize that much of what passes for Christian service or dedication is quite inadequate and shallow should take the initiative and direct the efforts of all, including the musicians and congregation, into meaningful praise and worship.

Praise was one of the primary features of the early Pentecost church. What is so notable about that feature is that it was so different from the legal, dour, and mundane religion which was always intent on criticizing and curtailing Christ's ministry of hope. The Jewish worship had, at one time, been beautiful; their Babylonian captors even wanted to hear them singing with their harps, and many of our songs today find inspiration in the Book of Psalms.

People need leaders who will educate them into the work of the Lord in their lives and in instructing them how to express their gratitude towards the Lord in praise. We are directed in Ephesians 5:19, 20:

[19]speaking to one another in psalms and hymns and spiritual songs, singing and making melody in your heart to the Lord,

[20]giving thanks always for all things to God the Father in the name of our Lord Jesus Christ

Luke 19:37–40 states the case for praise as an essential to our faith:

[37]Then, as He [Jesus] was now drawing near the descent of the Mount of Olives, the whole multitude of the disciples began to rejoice and praise God with a loud voice for all the mighty works they had seen,

[38]saying: "'*Blessed is the King who comes in the name of the Lord!*'

Peace in heaven and glory in the highest!"

[39]And some of the Pharisees called to Him from the crowd, "Teacher, rebuke Your disciples."

[40]But He answered and said to them, "I tell you that if these should be silent, the stones would immediately cry out."

Not only is praise a much-needed outlet for our faith, it is essentially a declaration of the victory and the greatness of God in a dark world lost in the despair of sin. Praise sets the devil back on his heels.

11. Kindness to Those Around

It was said of the early Christians by Tertullian, an early church father, "see how they love each other." His comment reflected the Christian's daily behavior among the pagan population.

Perhaps the overarching feature of the early church was its benevolent attitude to those around them. This included those outside their group, but also each other. So often our charitable deeds are directed to those most needful in our estimation and a target for increasing our influence and even, perhaps, membership.

We often resist affecting those we consider to be unworthy or less deserving or who might respond unfavorably towards us.

In the early Church, we have an example of unbiased generosity. Perhaps these folks considered "the hole of the pit from *whence* ye are digged" (Isaiah 51:1 KJV). Christians seem to be very adept at adopting a Pharisaical aloofness when it comes to dealing with the world. Especially, it is so for the "unclean" from whom we readily separate ourselves. Jesus didn't do this. He went among the lost to seek and save them.

Christian leadership should do all they can to instruct their membership of the duty and privilege of showing their light and demonstrating their gracious kindness; as one friend once replied to a co-worker who accused him of thinking he was better than him, "I don't think I'm better than you, but I think that, as a Christian, I am better off." Let us all take down our barriers of self-righteousness and self-importance we have erected against a messed-up world and simply shine our light.

Leaders have an opportunity to set the tone and direction for overcoming self-righteous barriers which are readily self-imposed. Sometimes our church doctrines and practices create these barriers, and we are horribly estranged from the world to whom we are called to present the redemption of the Lord Jesus.

It is amazing the change of attitude that the world portrays towards us when we restrain our judgmental attitude towards them. We begin to see them taking down their barriers when we get ours out of the way. They are our neighbors; we are to love them; they are not our enemies. (See Matthew 5:43–48.) Leaders need to instruct their members in this issue by example, program, and education.

12. Receiving New Members

The people at Jerusalem, and throughout the ancient world, who were convinced by all they heard and saw that Jesus was the Messiah, were also convinced that their religions of the day were inadequate. This is what gave them the confidence to cut their ties with formal religion and join themselves to the new church community.

It has historically been the case that those wishing to convert may sometimes fall away from their newfound faith or return to their roots because they have not been fully embraced into the new family of faith or are initially marginalized because of their cultural or economical differences.

Leadership must intentionally work to correct this failure by making provision through the allocation of resources and programs and the education of the people about how to receive into the fold those being "added by the Lord."

It is profoundly a worthy task for all levels of leadership in the church to make integration of their membership, their *Community of the Spirit,* a goal. "*Integrity*"; the word has, at its root, the sense of wholeness.

Sometimes the internal barriers and biases which people set up to protect their own sense of identity are profoundly cruel and do not follow Jesus's teaching but sow the seeds of division to be harvested at some later date.

Diversity in a community is not a threat to unity, but it is a profound strength when the exercise of that strength is properly directed towards a common purpose.

This common purpose and a fulsome annunciation is the work of the leadership ahead of every other competing agenda. In our churches, we are plagued with the promotion of personal and group agendas which so often try to piggyback the pure cause of Christ.

13. Sharing (Preaching and Teaching) the Gospel

It was this preaching of the gospel or the Apostle's doctrine which brought spiritual strength and understanding to this early church. It was a necessary strengthening process for the continuation of the cause of Christ. It also saved the new faith from degenerating and becoming just another religion based on mythology and ritual.

This preaching/teaching was a much-needed instrument to help deal with the rising heresies of Gnosticism. Every ambitious religious zealot seemed to be attracted to this growing *Community of the Spirit*. They sought to add, to the church's theology, their own brand of superstition and mysticism which was rooted in pagan practices.

The new church was indeed vulnerable to compromise and dilution of its theology and cause for Christ as these gnostic teachers went about to detract from the truth which the apostles had been given by their relationship with Christ.

God, providentially, had provided pastors who were commissioned to guard the truth by teaching the truth and condemning heresy.

Heresy is not just harmless optional thoughts, for it always seriously dilutes faith and the truth. Heresy will always introduce a sense of man's own work in legalistic practices and will make the man somewhat his own savior.

Today, in the church, our teaching lines of communication are rife with humanistic philosophy taught by educated men and women seeking an audience and support for their ambition to add to the body of Bible truth.

Modern day liberal teaching denies original sin in the individual and, instead, lays the blame for moral failure at the feet of society, for example.

The struggle today with philosophy is not a new issue. The early church fathers of the first and second century who were educated in Greek philosophy tried to view Christianity through the lens of their former teaching. Some notable errors and controversies in early Christian theology began to creep into the body of truth. After much struggle and debate, these tenets were eradicated for the most part. They are, however, present to seek a place in our modern theology.

The apostle's doctrine, which was shared in the *Community of the Spirit*, taught a personal responsibility for our state of sin and our acts of sin. This teaching advocates confession of sin and repentance and forgiveness through the shed blood of Christ as an antidote for sins' effects in our lives.

The goal of teaching should be to follow Biblical truths and lead to salvation instead of leaders seeking out answers for the human condition by the application of humanistic counseling.

14. Signs and Wonders

This vital feature of the early church, the *Community of the Spirit*, has been left to nearly the last, not because it is the least or less important, but because it is seen in scripture as a confirmation of the practice of the previous features just reviewed.

And they went out and preached everywhere, the Lord working with *them* and confirming the word through the accompanying signs (Mark 16:20).

The ministry of the early apostles was validated (or more correctly, their message of the resurrected Christ was validated) by signs and wonders:

God also bearing witness both with signs and wonders, with various miracles, and gifts of the Holy Spirit, according to His own will (Hebrews 2:4).

If the Lord still seeks to validate the preaching of truth by undeniable signs and wonders, then something must be amiss in our present church's motivation and message when we don't experience Biblical signs and wonders.

The question arises, do we preach Christ crucified for the redemption of sin? Or perhaps we tag onto the message a component of loyalty to the church implied as a necessary part of redemption. Or perhaps we teach the necessity of some requisite, legalistic works as an aid to inheriting eternal life. As well, many churches avoid profound expressions of emotion in favor of rational practice as a purer sign of faith. Regardless of our approach to preaching the "truth," the church is still in a deficit of credibility before the observing world. Often our attitudes of exclusion and separation, and of judgmental declarations, cause the world to reject our perceived gospel.

The early church had no religious program or rituals of dogmas to advance or to defend. The works of charity and a clear and profound witness of the resurrection was the program. Their gospel of inclusiveness and forgiveness of sins was unabashedly preached.

Can we expect God to provide signs and wonders of a supernatural nature as a result of our sectarian propagations?

It could be argued that God is always at work doing some degree of confirmation. We see answered prayers, changed lives, and healing of emotional hurts along the way. We have not yet, however, reached the place where observable, genuine signs and wonders in our western churches is regularly witnessed.

Christian leaders must newly examine whether our preaching of today is His gospel or more the case of our humanistic dialogues and machinations.

It is still possible to get to the place where true preaching of faith in His gospel produces the validity of signs and wonders. The original 15 features, mentioned previously, were the hallmarks of a vitalized Christian culture, pointing the direction out of the mire of modern mindsets found in many churches today.

15. Prayer

Prayer, the simple expression of faith's desires directed towards a caring God.

As leaders, there is an inherent responsibility to teach prayer and to make meaningful opportunity for the full expression of prayer in our spiritual community.

Prayer has been variously described by some as a desperate reaching towards a distant God or an expression of our base wishes directed towards an unknown force.

We have library shelves stocked with books defining how to pray effectively, how to pray to make our wishes realized, or even the most meaningful words to use in effective prayer.

The Acts 2 community seemed to pray instinctively and was also prompted by the Holy Spirit. They seemed to understand the meaning of these concepts:

—"men always ought to pray and not lose heart" (Luke 18:1); and,

— "pray without ceasing" (1 Thessalonians 5:17).

They prayed:

~ for the sick to recover.

They prayed:

~ for adequate resources to carry on day-to-day living.

They prayed:

~ for safety.

They prayed:

~ in the Spirit, and

They prayed:

~ with their understanding (1 Corinthians 14:15).

Prayer was not seen as a sidebar issue or a last-resort action.

Simply put, prayer was woven into the fabric of their everyday lives.

Prayer was an essential feature of the *Community of the Spirit* in every way. Prayer of faith makes the other fourteen (14) features, mentioned earlier, both workable and effective; oil for the machinery as it were.

Prayer binds us to God and His workings in our life.

As leaders, genuine prayer needs to be modeled and taught to followers of Christ. When we resist praying as a proper part of our Christian experience, any number of distractions will occupy our interest and our time.

Simple prayers are as effective as profound words if they are expressed in faith.

Prayer can quietly resolve major problems or shake the prisons which are not of our own making (Acts 5:19), a case of a physical prison. And Matthew 8:28–33 states the case of two demonically imprisoned Gadarenes.

The Bible is full of instructions about prayer:

"Ask and it shall be given you" (Matthew 7:7).

"...how much more will your heavenly Father give good things to those who ask Him" (Matthew 7:11)?

"And whatever things you ask in prayer, believing, you will receive" (Matthew 21:22).

"Until now you have asked nothing in My name. Ask and you will receive that your joy may be full" (John 16:24).

- Prayer is not the influential prevue of the holy.
- Prayer is the effective resource of the sanctified.
- Prayer is the oxygen of the *Community of the Spirit*.

We are not so much instructed how to pray, or when to pray; but we are instructed just to pray—always.

Effective prayer is most effectively taught by modeling it rather than by talking about it.

Issues to be Evaluated and Corrected by Leadership

The adoption and accommodation of the Acts 2 Model into any modern church curriculum will, of necessity, require adjustments to our practices and the formation of new values. To achieve this goal, the organization will be required to adjust its self-image and re-evaluate the organizational purposes, not as a resource to maintain and advance its own interests, but rather, it should see itself as a renewed place to invest wisdom and grace into the working body. This Acts 2 adopted model will transform the *Community of the Spirit* into a force that will go on into a sinful world that is doomed to hellfire.

A radical "slash and burn" approach is not what is required at this point. Rather, a sober evaluation, not a criticism of the Church's ministry efforts, should be undertaken. Prayer and reflection along with communication which is open and honest will be required.

The following issues must first be carefully evaluated and corrected:

1. Confidence and Encouragement
    All people of the pews do not sit with a tank full of dedicated motivation ready to go. Guilt and shame will do nothing to get them to the starting line. Often after years of safe pew-tending, people need a large supply of confidence and encouragement in both their task to be completed and the Lord's readiness to direct their sincere efforts.

Confidence among the people is required to be taught and demonstrated.

2. Ability

We are not all of the same ability to undertake any or all tasks which may be assigned. It is surprising that often "a soft answer will turn away wrath" (Proverbs 15:1) is needed and should be appreciated in preference to a bold communicator of talents. There is a place for everyone in spite of our human evaluation and grading of talents which often places little significance on the very treasures that God wants to use. There are no stars in God's plan. He rewards faith and obedience.

3. Training

We are not all biblically or emotionally prepared to undertake all ministry tasks. We all need to be trained in whatever task may lie before us. It's about "some sowing and some reaping." Winning is not essential; just shining your light of witness and testimony is essential. Leave the results to God. Don't statistically hog-tie your efforts. Training to identifiable tasks is important. An honest evaluation of where we are at and what we must do to correct our deficits will be needed to establish a training curriculum.

4. Opportunity

"A word fitly spoken *is like* apples of gold in settings of silver" (Proverbs 25:11). Opportunities to shine are everywhere around us. We shine by showing grace in gesture and word, and these actions are a reflection of our salt and light. We need to demonstrate who we are more than what we believe. Doctrine will never win the day over character. Opportunity is what we make of it.

5. Leadership

Leaders must never demean the good intentions or good works of believers. Leaders should not favor quick successes. Many successful actions of sowing require time to reach a suitable harvest. Often the process goes on unheralded or even unheeded. Whether our actions are rebuffed or ridiculed, it is of no consequence. When we exert ourselves for the Lord, we have put the seed into the care of the Holy Spirit who will use our efforts as He wills. It is often surprising what will take down the dark barriers of resistance to the gospel.

Jesus said, "Let your light so shine before men that they may see your good works and glorify your Father in heaven" (Matthew 5:16).

6. Celebrate

Leaders should always celebrate and encourage the sincere efforts of believers who attempt to shine their lights into dark places. Celebrate these efforts vigorously and openly. The first discovered feature of the New Testament church was gladness (Acts 2:41). We are never to be seen as victims as we go obediently about the task of shining our lights before men. The unbelievers are the victims who believe the lies of the devil.

7. Encourage

   Any effort to shine your light is a worthy one. We live in a time of superstar adulation. When we applaud these "rock stars," we are living vicariously. Too soon, we cease to appreciate our own worthy tasks and, instead, adulate and idolize the talented and famous. Too soon, we become followers of men instead of followers of Christ. It seems the best place to idolize the stars is from our pews. We have so readily borrowed this perversion from the world and made it our own. Jesus never taught or demonstrated such a system of religious glorification or the performers in the church. Acts 2 never postulated such a stance either.

Assessment of Present Church Initiatives

Christian leaders must honestly ask, can we expect God to bless efforts which are largely about serving and enlarging our own religious institutions?

Oh, the gilded bushels that we choose to raise up as our idols! How embellished are the bushels we choose to hide our light? Where is the light? Jesus said that we are the light of the world (Matthew 5:14). Can we, at this time in the various western Church cultures and development, choose more meaningful methods of outreach for *the Community of the Spirit* ministries just as the early Christians did? The efforts we undertake will be a measure of our obedience to Him.

Leadership and layperson alike, who are involved in Christian activities, should create a plan for the evaluation of their own Church activities and work through their issues. To help with this and for your consideration, I have created a list of suggested evaluation issues following this section. Those who have become pew-tenders need to consider that a dormant or an entrenched stance on Christian service is not a Biblical option and is fraught with a Laodicea judgment in the end (Revelation 3:17). We cannot, in good conscience, focus only on our issues while the world proceeds into destruction without our witness to the truth of salvation.

Because you say, "I am rich, have become wealthy, and have need of nothing"—and do not know that you are wretched, miserable, poor, blind, and naked (Revelation 3:17).

Many church growth programs are assessed against some working models which are deemed to be successful. Usually these models espouse values such as attendance and offerings. However, the outpouring of the Holy Spirit on Pentecost, the model we have been reviewing, is an original model unblemished by today's secular values and is a worthy model for Christian leadership to evaluate their present church programs against. The blessing of God is our desired outcome, not quantitative rewards. It is also an effective model to help us to realize the results of the expenditure of our energies and resources.

Action Events for Christian Leaders

1. Undertake an **assessment** of your present philosophy and practice against the Acts 2 Model. Remember, honesty is a valuable virtue in resolving outstanding problems. A council of leaders may be used to help; however, the leader, as an individual, should resolve to personally undertake this exercise first. Perhaps it would be also helpful if participating leaders would do their own evaluation of their personal life priorities.

2. Enter into **confession** before a graceful Lord for the discrepancies found in your own personal evaluation and then proceed to deal with these discrepancies openly and honestly before God.

3. **Repentance** is hard, that is, true repentance which will evoke change; but an open and honest repentance without excuses will relieve you of the weight of past failures and will prevent you carrying dead weight into the future or returning to past errors.

4. A **realignment** of purpose and **reassignment** of resources will be required of the leadership. Turn the ship of faith around. Craft a new ministerial plan and, in it, reference the Acts 2 features identified in your new ministry plan. How can these features be best communicated and practiced in your church activities?

5. **Instruction** and **Communication** is a necessary and often missing component in church activities and ventures. Do it well and often with everyone affected. Don't assume that people "get it" the first time around. You may be surprised, however, at the genuine response and support. The volunteer base will be activated by your honest evaluation and plans.

6. In **implementing** a remedial action plan, dismantling and realignment may be necessary as you discover and discuss the "sacred cows" that have been adopted and that do not serve your new intentions.

7. Now onward to the **Go and Do**. However feeble or infantile your actions seem to be, and regardless of how objectionable these new values and actions may appear to special interest groups, **do** them as unto the Lord. Always cover your actions with **prayer**.

8. From time to time, in order to avoid drift into old patterns, it will be necessary to **re-evaluate** outcomes and to **affirm** success, in particular, to those who eagerly pursue these new ventures and values. Evaluation input should be received from all parties affected by these new values and ventures.

9. You will need to be prepared to have the strength for **redoubling efforts**. Whenever weaknesses and lack of enthusiasm is encountered, it will be necessary for the leadership to employ new methods of implementation or personnel to continually improve your outcomes.

10. You will have the awesome privilege of **giving God the Glory**. Celebrate success and acknowledge God's good grace in overcoming redundancy and for achieving Biblical goals in your church life.
    For your convenience:

Objective commentary and commitment often allows us to evaluate our understanding and helps to set our sights on new goals of endeavor. The following evaluation forms taken individually or collectively provide a benchmark to your goals. Often a group exercise will furnish an opportunity for dialogue which may lead to a collective undertaking.

A score of 3 or less should indicate a need for corrective action personally or corporately as suits the case.

Leadership Evaluation of
<u>Church</u>
Actions Page 1 of 4
Date: _____
M D Y

VALUES

List four or more values which are <u>apparent</u> in your local church and rate them 1 to 5 in their effectiveness and vigor.

  Scale:
  1 —least evident, lacking vigor
  2 —somewhat effective, some vigor
  3 —satisfactory, but needs improvement
  4 —effective and vigorous
  5 —excelling expectations, very effective with great vigor

<u>RATE</u> (circle)

....
....1 2 3 4 5
....
....1 2 3 4 5
....
....1 2 3 4 5

....

....1 2 3 4 5

....

....1 2 3 4 5

....

....1 2 3 4 5

Comments

....

....

....

....

....

....

ORDER

List what methodology your church has <u>in place</u> to deliver these values to their place of need. Rate their effectiveness.

Scale:
1 —ineffective
2 —somewhat effective
3 —satisfactory, needs improvement
4 —good results
5 —exceeds expectations

<u>RATE</u> (circle)

....
....1 2 3 4 5
....
....1 2 3 4 5
....
....1 2 3 4 5
....
....1 2 3 4 5
....
....1 2 3 4 5
....
....1 2 3 4 5
....
....1 2 3 4 5

Comments

....
....
....
....
....
....

STRUCTURE

List the application of order that you have adopted in your organization. Does the practice of this order demonstrate a general congregational demeanor and agreement with the espoused values?

Scale:
1 —no observable agreement
2 —some demonstration of agreement
3 —conditional agreement
4 —majority demonstrate agreement
5 —order understood and agreement established

<u>RATE</u> (circle)

....
....1 2 3 4 5

....
....1 2 3 4 5

....
....1 2 3 4 5

....
....1 2 3 4 5

....
....1 2 3 4 5

....
....1 2 3 4 5

....
....1 2 3 4 5

Comments

....
....
....
....

Leadership Evaluation of
<u>Church</u>
Actions Page 4 of 4

CAUSE
What cause or causes drive the efforts of your activities?

Scale:
    1 —drives no activities
    2 —drives few
    3 —often drives
    4 —usually drives
    5 —mostly drives activities

<u>RATE</u> (circle)

....
....1 2 3 4 5
....
....1 2 3 4 5
....
....1 2 3 4 5
....
....1 2 3 4 5
....
....1 2 3 4 5
....
....1 2 3 4 5

Comments:
....
....
....
....
....
....
....
....

Leadership Evaluation of
<u>Personal Conduct</u>
Page 1 of 4

Date: _____

M D Y

VALUES

Rank your <u>personal</u> values as a Christian Leader; the values you attempt to serve. Rate your perceived effectiveness in establishing these in your ministry and personal life.

Scale:
- 1 —lack effectiveness
- 2 —somewhat effective, establishing phase
- 3 —satisfactory, improving
- 4 —good effectiveness
- 5 —most effective

Ministry   **Personal**

................................1 2 3 4 5   ....1 2 3 4 5

................................1 2 3 4 5   ....1 2 3 4 5

................................1 2 3 4 5   ....1 2 3 4 5

................................1 2 3 4 5   ....1 2 3 4 5

................................1 2 3 4 5   ....1 2 3 4 5

Comments

....
....
....
....
....
....
....
....
....
....

ORDER Has an effective order been established by <u>habitual practice</u> in carrying these values to fruition?

Scale:
    1 —not established
    2 —sporadic, experimenting
    3 —less sporadic
    4 — habitual
    5 —fully established

Ministry   **Personal**

...............................1 2 3 4 5   ....1 2 3 4 5

...............................1 2 3 4 5   ....1 2 3 4 5

...............................1 2 3 4 5   ....1 2 3 4 5

...............................1 2 3 4 5   ....1 2 3 4 5

...............................1 2 3 4 5   ....1 2 3 4 5

Comments
....
....
....
....
....
....
....
....
....
....

STRUCTURE

Rate the personal structure available/exercised by you as you utilize a volunteer system.

Scale:
1 —no structure or guidelines in place
2 —structure available, but not exercised
3 —structure in place and sometimes exercised
4 —structure routinely exercised
5 —structure exercised and excellent communication established

Ministry	**Personal**
...............................1 2 3 4 5	...............................1 2 3 4 5
...............................1 2 3 4 5	...............................1 2 3 4 5
...............................1 2 3 4 5	...............................1 2 3 4 5
...............................1 2 3 4 5	...............................1 2 3 4 5
...............................1 2 3 4 5	...............................1 2 3 4 5

Comments
....
....
....
....
....
....
....
....
....
....

CAUSE

What cause or causes personally drive your efforts in service to the body of believers?

Scale:
1 —I avoid this (comments below)
2 —drives few efforts
3 —often drives efforts
4 —usually drives efforts
5 —mostly drives efforts

Ministry Personal

Ministry	Personal
..................................1 2 3 4 5	..................................1 2 3 4 5
..................................1 2 3 4 5	..................................1 2 3 4 5
..................................1 2 3 4 5	..................................1 2 3 4 5
..................................1 2 3 4 5	..................................1 2 3 4 5
..................................1 2 3 4 5	..................................1 2 3 4 5

Comments
....
....
....
....
....
....
....

~ PART TEN ~

Pew Tenders Arise

The responsibilities of Christian leadership have been addressed previously in Part 3. Any modern practitioner in the church will realize that change is not always readily received by all parties. However, now let us address the opportunities and the responsibilities afforded those who I earlier identified as "the pew-tenders." I used that term because of what is apparent in many churches; many people prefer to attend church rather than participate, an option Jesus did not consider a worthy way to live a Christian life.

[13] "You are the salt of the earth; but if the salt loses its flavor, how shall it be seasoned? It is then good for nothing but to be thrown out and trampled underfoot by men.

[14] You are the light of the world. A city that is set on a hill cannot be hidden.

[15] Nor do they light a lamp and put it under a basket, but on a lampstand, and it gives light to all *who are* in the house.

[16] Let your light so shine before men, that they may see your good works and glorify your Father in heaven" (Matthew 5:13–16).

What we desperately need today is some remedial force that will bring the whole church into a new phase of health and effectiveness through meaningful activity. The coming of the Holy Spirit was that agent of change in the first century.

We must identify our defective methodology which has created a church in our own image.

We must find a way of modern reformation which would provide a more responsible means of ministry. This correction methodology must be able to fit into any church wishing to become a more relevant and dynamic church for these last days.

This work does not espouse a one-size-fits-all remedy. Remember that the model of Acts 2 can be taken and customized according to present church mission. The model is amenable to every minister and to every worship style and denomination which calls itself Christian. This action is not a legalistic program; however, the Fifteen Features of Acts 2 can fully provide us with an adequate roadmap to begin our journey.

In our day-to-day walk of faith with the Lord, to our loss, we are often observed by the world based on what we do not do rather than what we do. All good intentions aside, the world we seek to save judges the content of our salt and light endeavors. However, the notable feature of *the Community of the Spirit* in our, often referenced, Acts 2 Model was energized by the Holy Spirit. This early church body was not known by its negative actions, as were the Pharisees which Jesus interacted with, but was known for what it did do—the positive actions. These negative actions demonstrate our adherence to the law or our vaunted dogmas, not the freedom of faith which Christ's sacrifice has provided to the world to enjoy. We know that God is working out His plan for history, but He has enlisted all believers in the honorable position of being witnesses of His grace by *"going and doing."*

These recorded actions of charity, piety, and faith, as recorded for us in Acts 2, were unordinary in that time of religious bigotry and legalism. These new attitudes of *the Community of the Spirit* and their actions of grace and charity broke from the prevailing religious traditions, but in doing so, they did not break any civil or religious laws. The affect was profoundly changing to the culture. History has shown that real Christianity has always been a force of change.

Today, much of our religious energy, material resources, and human resources are spent within the confines of our denominational dictates and expectations. We are seen to practice a very *"no risk, play it safe"* program of church actions that are, to a large extent, self-serving. Like the children's chorus of past times said, "I'm on the inside, on which side are you?" People who are on the outside of God's love and forgiveness don't need reminding; they need help. The gospel in our hands is the remedy if we care to take it "outside" our walk.

We also have become, to a large extent, spectators of Christian leaders who entertain us or perform ritual and liturgy for our observance. However, we are poorly sanctified and edified by these religious displays, and our placid approval bears no eternal fruit.

We come away from these Sunday events having paid our dues and extended our smiles and good feelings to fellow celebrants. We feel that we have appeased our expected responsibilities or sense of responsibility for the time being, like the ancient Jews who had been forever obligated to repeated sacrifices but had left the temple with the same heart that they came in with. And they had left the temple with the same burden of sin to contend with and as they had been burdened with when they had arrived.

The church conduct which we witness from week to week has its roots largely as a result of the changes which occurred in the Church of Rome by

Constantine's nod of approval (313 AD). Some scholars refer to this time as "the Captivity." Enough cannot be said about how this captivity has kept the laity submissive and largely dormant, even in today's church.

Perhaps the worst action taken was the wholesale seizure of ministry by the Roman Church and the exclusion of lay ministry as it had been practiced since Pentecost. It was a notable effort to keep the lay people ignorant and suppressed and the Roman government approved of a quiet citizenship. This suppression of the docile church was with the government support. The practice of state churches has always been to maintain a passive laity in order to gain support from the state.

Throughout the time of captivity until the Reformation, scripture was forbidden to be made available to the church membership. Persecution soon rose up against those who sought to read or teach the Bible truths.

This persecution continued to suppress true faith in the Bible until the Reformation of Luther (1483–1546) and Tyndale (1494–1536) when faith was released, largely by the dissemination of the written Bible in the vernacular.

However, the Reformation did not cause the total evacuation and cleansing from pagan and Roman practices in the Church.

The order of rule and control still continued by virtue of dogma, ritual, and liturgy, which in some cases was little changed.

The priesthood or clergy were still seen to be the only legitimate dispensers of grace and benefice to the congregation. Many enthusiastic believers were persecuted by the newly formed church, and they were martyred because of their preaching of Bible truths. John 1:17 tells us "the law was given through Moses, *but* grace and truth came through Jesus Christ."

The holding of the *franchise of faith* and grace was maintained in many forms from those days and is present today. *Franchise of faith* meant that access to God was only available through the Church's grace and sacraments; personal faith, as the Bible taught, was held to be meaningless. Affirmation and approval were still largely conditioned upon conformation to the established Church norms of denominational doctrine and dogma.

Our study of Acts 2, as a witness of the empowerment of the Holy Spirit, rejects much of what we have come to in church practices today. We expect religious correctness, and the Acts 2 church practiced Holy Spirit empowerment.

This *Community of the Spirit* demonstrated no sense of conditional approval or qualification to be required for participation in ministry or for charitable activities. There is no formal sense of rulership, no formal clerical hierarchy or control to be found here. How the pure energy of the Holy Spirit moves us towards self-effacing service to our fellow man when we submit to His wooing.

This pure action of charity and the power of faith is repeated historically again and again as the Holy Spirit revivals of faith occurred through the centuries. Not many great churches or cathedrals were built as a result of response to the Holy Spirit, but the Acts 2 *Community of the Spirit* was revived on every occasion. Many edifices of worship are built as memorials to men and the power of the Church. Grace was received from God throughout these Holy Spirit revivals.

So we are reminded that the Bible declares; "we are all called according to His purpose" (Romans 8:28).

Further, I Corinthians 1:26–29 declares our responsibility and state:

²⁶For you see your calling, brethren, that not many wise according to the flesh, not many mighty, not many noble are called.

²⁷But God has chosen the foolish thing of this world to put to shame the wise, and God has chosen the weak things of the world to put to shame the things that are mighty,

²⁸And the base things of the world and the things which are not, to bring to nothing the things which are.

²⁹That no flesh should glory in His presence.

The mighty rule of the Roman Empire was destroyed from within; its ruthless pagan character softened by the gospel of grace. Many scholars agree that the energy and the character of the early Christian church, which began on Pentecost and continued until Constantine's rule, was largely to blame; for it brought to bear Christian love and charity into the heart of the Roman citizens by the multitude of faithful witnesses.

The effects of a "Holy Spirit" energized church, in any age, will cause evil to be put down and righteousness to be exalted. Today, we need that energy to work through our outreach ministries and the *Community of the Spirit*. We are, after all, referred to as "*salt and light*"—game changers.

Of late, a new slogan has been put forth in the church and its membership. That often heard slogan is "*Stand Up*." For too many years, the "church" has been invisible or intimidated, affecting no real change in our society. We have been afraid to carry the witness of *salt and light* outside of our safe, self-imposed boundaries, our church walls.

Profound and positive change in the culture has always been the outcome; profound, positive change is the fruit of an energized church.

The *gilded bushel* has been our most prominent hiding place; whether it has been our psychology of church practices and purposes or doctrinal dogma and hierarchy which has given us a convenient opportunity to lay back and to let the professionals *do* the ministry. These practices cannot be found Biblically; pew tenders are not given *a pass* on the action.

We cannot continue to hide as the much prophesied "government resistance and persecution" comes against the church. We must come out from behind our imposed bushels and let our individual light shine (Matthew 5:16). Let the church be the church.

We will find that the most meaningful affirmation is not to be found in our ecclesiastical approvals and comfort, but, in the end, the "well done, thou good and faithful servant" (Matthew 25:21, KJV). It will be Jesus who pronounces this benediction, Jesus the Righteous Judge who will declare as we give account for our lives on that day when we stand before His throne. We bow our heads to our everlasting shame if obedience has not been taken up in preference over the accolades of our generation of pew-tenders.

Once again, the call to those who "spectate" rather than participate has not been rescinded in our days.

Let a man so consider us, as servants [ministers] of Christ and stewards of the mysteries of God (1 Corinthians 4:1).

Not that we are sufficient of ourselves to think of anything as *being* from ourselves, but our sufficiency *is* from God, who also made us sufficient [able] as ministers of the new covenant, not of the letter but of the Spirit; for the letter kills, but the Spirit gives life (2 Corinthians 3:5,6).

~ PART ELEVEN ~

Manifesto of Faith

There is a place of balance to be discovered in our Christian walk of faith.

We seem drawn to a place of affirmation by our peers and our institution. This approval comes at the expense of laying aside our own personal walk with the Lord, as our freedom of faith will always direct us away from all that is religiously imposed. But we need to step out of our much-averred comfort zones.

Paul describes his journey to faith in Philippians 3:7–11:

⁷But what things were gain to me, these I have counted loss for Christ.

⁸Yet indeed I also count all things loss for the excellence of the knowledge of Christ Jesus my Lord, for whom I have suffered loss of all things, and count them as rubbish, that I may gain Christ

⁹and be found in Him, not having my own righteousness, which *is* from the law, but that which *is* through faith in Christ, the righteousness which is from God by faith;

¹⁰that I may know Him and the power of His resurrection, and the fellowship of His sufferings, being conformed to His death,

¹¹if, by any means, I may attain to the resurrection from the dead.

Especially, you will note verse nine, "and be found in Him, not having my own righteousness, which *is* from the law, but that which *is* through faith in Christ, the righteousness which is from God by faith."

Abraham also journeyed towards righteousness as he followed God's direction. Abraham did not have the benefit of written scriptures or a priesthood to follow, nor did he have any religious system to direct his life. Simply, as Genesis 15:6 states, "And he [Abraham] believed in the LORD, and He accounted it to him for righteousness." His relationship with God was such that God spoke to him and Abraham heard Him; a place of sensitivity that we, also, should seek today. God chooses to speak today through the written word and His still small voice.

Abraham's faith in God alone led him through many challenges to become the covenanted father of all who are of faith in the LORD. His faith, just as Paul's faith, aside from the distraction of religious law, found them both on an acceptable standing before God. That standing, of course, was righteousness before a Holy God.

Paul's faith and Abraham's faith was not just a "said" faith, but because they believed God, their faith was dynamic. As we, like the people of Dostoyevsky's tale mentioned earlier, lay down our freedom which faith brings us, we are led to a place of submissive subjection to contrived order and religious duty. The problem with that submissive status is that it does not require faith and is unrewarded by God's approval. We, instead, trade our living faith for a pew-tender's docility. We also assume a small risk as we follow and don't assume any form of adventurous faith. We simply accept the mystery, miracle, and authority provided by the operations of a political, religious system and have no need for a personal active faith. Sadly, we are found congratulating each other in our empty achievements.

The Roman Church has exercised a system wherein they are the sole source of allotted faith and grace. The adherent's personal faith has no place in the system except as it is placed as faith in the faith of the Church. It's easy to ridicule such a system, but we non-Romans are essentially doing the same thing when we do not personally "fight the good fight of faith," but are satisfied to become subjective pew-tenders (1 Timothy 6:12). We easily are found serving our chosen or imposed religious system rather than following Christ as He leads us into the market place of need and service.

As we have begun our walk of faith in the beginning of our religious journey, we must continue to see all religious benefices as a role of support for our faith in the edification, instruction, and exhortation such Churches are designed to offer.

Although we may acquiesce to religious pressures, however subtle they may be, we still must answer to the Lord for our conduct of personal faith in Him at our time before His throne. There does not seem to be any reward in heaven for sheep-like pew-tenders.

Hebrews 11:6:

But without faith *it is* impossible to please *Him*, for he who comes to God must believe that He is, and *that* He is a rewarder of those who diligently seek Him.

Hebrews 11:32–40, NIV:

[32] And what more shall I say? I do not have time to tell about Gideon, Barak, Samson, Jephthah, David, Samuel and the prophets,

[33] who through faith conquered kingdoms, administered justice, and gained what was promised; who shut the mouths of lions,

³⁴quenched the fury of the flames, and escaped the edge of the sword; whose weakness was turned to strength; who became powerful in battle and routed foreign armies.

³⁵Women received back their dead, raised to life again. Others were tortured and refused to be released, so that they might gain a better resurrection.

³⁶Some faced jeers and flogging, while still others were chained and put in prison.

³⁷They were stoned; they were sawed in two; they were put to death by the sword. They went about in sheepskins and goatskins, destitute, persecuted, and mistreated—

³⁸the world was not worthy of them. They wandered in deserts and mountains, and in caves and holes in the ground.

³⁹These were all commended for their faith, yet none of them received what had been promised.

⁴⁰God had planned something better for us so that only together with us would they be made perfect.

> Faith is the issue of relationship with God;
> not a "said" faith,
> not a faith arrived at some time ago;
> but a vital, ongoing, "get up off your seats" faith,
> a faith that has an imperative attached to it,
> a faith that entails risk of goods and reputation,
> a faith like Christ demonstrated.

Hebrews 12:2, NIV:

Let us fix our eyes on Jesus, the author and perfecter of our faith, who for the joy set before him endured the cross, scorning its shame, and sat down at the right hand of the throne of God.

Jesus did not pontificate on an earthly throne of religious making, but endured:

²¹To this you were called, because Christ suffered for you, leaving you an example, that you should follow in his steps.

²²"He committed no sin, and no deceit was found in his mouth" (Isaiah 53:9).

²³When they hurled their insults at him, he did not retaliate; when he suffered, he made no threats. Instead, he entrusted himself to him who judges justly.

²⁴He himself bore our sins in his body on the tree, so that we might die to sins and live for righteousness; by his wounds you have been healed (I Peter 2:21–24, NIV).

We can take direction and inspiration from Hebrews 12:1–28:

¹Therefore we also, since we are surrounded by so great a cloud of witnesses, let us lay aside every weight, and the sin which so easily ensnares *us*, and **let us run with endurance the race that is set before us,**

²**looking unto Jesus**, the author and finisher of *our* faith, who for the joy that was set before Him endured the cross, despising the shame, and sat down at the right hand of the throne of God.

³For consider Him who endured such hostility from sinners against Himself, **lest you become weary and discouraged in your souls.**

⁴**You have not yet resisted to bloodshed, striving against sin.**

⁵And **you have forgotten the exhortation** which speaks to you as to sons:

"My son, do not despise the chastening of the LORD,

Nor be discouraged when you are rebuked by Him;

⁶For whom the LORD loves He chastens,

And scourges every son whom He receives."

⁷If you endure chastening, God deals with you as sons; for what son is there whom a father does not chasten?

⁸But if you are without chastening, of which all have become partakers, then you are illegitimate and not sons.

⁹Furthermore, we have had human fathers who corrected *us*, and we paid *them* respect. Shall we not much more readily be in subjection to the Father of spirits and live?

¹⁰For they indeed for a few days chastened *us* as seemed *best* to them, but He for *our* profit, that we may be partakers of His holiness.

¹¹Now no chastening seems to be joyful for the present, but painful; nevertheless, afterward it yields the peaceable fruit of righteousness to those who have been trained by it.

¹²Therefore strengthen the hands that hang down, and the feeble knees,

¹³and make straight paths for your feet, so that what is lame may not be *dislocated*, but rather be healed.

¹⁴Pursue peace with all *people*, and holiness, without which no one will see the Lord:

¹⁵looking carefully lest anyone fall short of the grace of God; lest any root of bitterness springing up cause trouble, and by this many become defiled;

¹⁶lest there *be* any fornicator or profane person like Esau, who for one morsel of food sold his birthright.

¹⁷For you know that afterward, when he wanted to inherit the blessing, he was rejected, for he found no place for repentance, though he sought it diligently with tears.

¹⁸For you have not come to the mountain that may be touched and that burned with fire, and to blackness and darkness and tempest,

¹⁹and the sound of a trumpet and the voice of words, so that those who heard *it* begged that the word should not be spoken to them anymore.

²⁰(For they could not endure what was commanded: "*And if so much as a beast touches the mountain, it shall be stoned for shot with an arrow.*"

²¹And so terrifying was the sight that Moses said, "*I am exceedingly afraid and trembling.*")

²²But you have come to Mount Zion and to the city of the living God, the heavenly Jerusalem, to an innumerable company of angels,

²³to the general assembly and church of the firstborn *who are* registered in heaven, to God the Judge of all, to the spirits of just men made perfect,

²⁴to Jesus the Mediator of the new covenant, and to the blood of sprinkling that speaks better things than *that of* Abel.

²⁵See that you do not refuse Him who speaks. For if they did not escape who refused Him who spoke on earth, much more *shall we not escape* if we turn away from Him who *speaks* from heaven,

²⁶whose voice then shook the earth; but now He has promised, saying, "*Yet once more I shake not only the earth, but also heaven.*"

²⁷Now this, "*Yet once more,*" indicates the removal of those things that are being shaken, as of things that are made, that the things which cannot be shaken may remain.

²⁸Therefore, since we are receiving a kingdom which cannot be shaken, let us have grace, by which we may serve God acceptably with reverence and godly fear.

²⁹For our God is a consuming fire.

And we will then become an effective *salt and light* witness which will cause change so profoundly needed in our time.

Unified resistance to sin and tyranny is always identified by people who participate in such resistance. They are known for their actions of faith and charity. They are also known for their stand on issues against evil. A group of resisters has no anonymity. There is no safety from risk, except as the body of resisters represent a notable mass of population. But, if we are to be joined by others of a like dynamic faith, we each must stand up with an agenda of righteousness, not religion, and we each must be careful to act within the dynamic of faith not institutional persuasion.

God's pure word sets the standard of faith which lives in each of us by His Spirit. If we are to succeed for future generations, we must now "*Stand Up for Jesus.*"

Push Back the Darkness, Let Your Bright Light Shine

We are encouraged, even commanded, to stand up with the word of God in hand.

2 Chronicles 17:9, 10:

[9]So they [the teaching priests] taught in Judah, and *had* the Book of the Law of the LORD with them; they went throughout all the cities of Judah and taught the people.

[10]And the fear of the LORD fell on all the kingdoms of the lands that *were* around Judah, so that they did not make war against Jehoshaphat.

2 Chronicles 15:7:

"But you, be strong and do not let your hands be weak, for your work shall be rewarded!"

Philippians 2:14–16:

[14]Do all things without complaining and disputing,

[15]that you may become blameless and harmless, children of God without fault in the midst of a crooked and perverse generation, among whom you shine as lights in the world,

[16]holding fast the word of life, so that I may rejoice in the day of Christ that I have not run in vain or labored in vain.

Colossians 3:12–17:

[12]Therefore, as *the* elect of God, holy and beloved, put on tender mercies, kindness, humility, meekness, longsuffering;

[13]bearing with one another, and forgiving one another, if anyone has a complaint against another; even as Christ forgave you, so you also *must do*.

[14]But above all these things put on love, which is the bond of perfection.

[15]And let the peace of God rule in your hearts, to which also you were called in one body; and be thankful.

[16]Let the word of Christ dwell in you richly in all wisdom, teaching and admonishing one another in psalms and hymns and spiritual songs, singing with grace in your hearts to the Lord.

[17]And *whatever* you do in word or deed, *do* all in the name of the Lord Jesus, giving thanks to God the Father through Him.

2 Timothy 4:1–5:

[1]I charge you therefore before God and the Lord Jesus Christ, who will judge the living and dead at His appearing and His kingdom:

[2]Preach the word! Be ready in season *and* out of season. Convince, rebuke, exhort, with all longsuffering and teaching.

[3]For the time will come when they will not endure sound doctrine, but according to their own desires, *because* they have itching ears, they will heap up for themselves teachers;

[4]and they will turn *their* ears away from the truth and be turned aside to fables.

[5]But you be watchful in all things, endure afflictions, do the work of an evangelist, fulfil your ministry.

The witness of "salt and light" to this present generation is woefully deficient. Such a witness is not ever completed by the church's opulence or cultural influence. The soldiers of the cross, the redeemed, the *Community of the Spirit*, in each age, is charged with the responsibility of "so shining" their light (Matthew 5:16).

Therefore, this discourse is, if you will, a "call to arms" for the pew-tenders, to step up their life force and shine.

So then, "Pew-Tenders Arise!"

Postscript

The purpose of the foregoing commentary is to highlight the force of the witness that was provided to the new *Community of the Spirit*. When the Holy Spirit was lavishly poured out on and *poured into* the believers on the day of Pentecost, a new range of experience and participation of the believers began.

This *Community of the Spirit* of that time no longer looked to the religious elite to practice the fundamentals of the Mosaic Law and the traditions which were developed after the Babylonian captivity. These men and women were a vital force in the coming of the kingdom of Heaven. They became the witnesses of salt and light in the gospel's redemption work of salvation. That's the point here; we are called as witnesses, not observers.

~~~~

This discourse has examined the early church behavior, the church of the Lord's making, that was empowered by the Holy Spirit. We have seen the profound effectiveness and the zeal of the early *Community of the Spirit*. We have tried to describe the features of the church listing the Fifteen Features as found in Acts 2. We have also revealed the action that is necessary by the actions of leaders to recover the authenticity of this *Community of the Spirit*. The whole point of this treatise is to return the modern Church to a place which will impact the societies we live in.

In raising the shortcomings between the *Community of the Spirit* being a living witness and a dormant observer, it was not the intent of this work to highlight any denomination or its doctrines as the source of these problems. The Roman Church (specifically) is mentioned because outright ambition and presumption drove these religious men of old times to try to assume the kingdom of Heaven. However, the state of faith in the Christian community of our own country today provides enough opportunity for blame to be assumed by us all, Church and laity.

Today, we face the poor health of our witness and we all must stand up to the challenges and opposition which faith puts before us.

"Now faith is the substance [realization] of things hoped for, the evidence [confidence] of things not seen" (Hebrews 11:1).

Faith, not practices and dogmas.

It has often been postulated or prophesied that the present ascent of the humanistic state will soon clash with Christian values and morals. It will soon categorize Christian values as hatemongering and will be able to impose penalties to suit their agenda. An aggressive *"Onward Christian Soldiers"* action by the Church into the marketplace of the lost and unsaved will demonstrate the strength and intention of *the Community of the Spirit* in positively affecting society's sickness and will change the Church's stance. Large congregations of socially and spiritually inactive people offer no resistance to the state's humanistic agenda.

Remember, the culture has never been the friend of the Church, the *Community of the Spirit.*

APPENDIX 1

The Woman at the Well

If she came to our church
With husbands, children and all
Would they fit our molds?
Would they clash with schemes?

Dress codes found habits carried
With husbands, children and all
Would their acts abuse our peace?
Would "saved from sin" do for us?

Rejection, pain, censure their lot
Acceptance, healing approval their quest
Would this be easy or would we recoil?
Would His forgiveness be found in us?

Could we rally to this cause?
Set aside our sense of right
Would we squeeze them to the side?
Or reach with charity as we were found

Would "all things new" be seen by us?
As part of the present not seeing the past
How beautiful the repentant seem to be
To our Father who found us in our own sin

John B. (Jack) Duncan

Passing by on the Other Side

After all
Shouldn't we? Indeed we do
Congratulate our attempts at simple greatness
We've achieved the things that men applaud
And in our eyes, their eyes, we look good
Receive the applause offered by men.

And yet unmarked, unsoiled by all
Human need, despair or plight
We easily pass by on the other side[5]
Applause intact, secured by looking good
Leaving behind doing good.

The parable falling on ears untouched
The Master's word "unto the least of these…"[1]
"As unto Me," ignored; applause in place
How shall we answer the revelators cry?
Wretched, miserable, poor, and blind and naked.[2]

Shall silent alms; our Father's reward[3]
Bear witness against us as deeds undone?
Shall the trump praise our cause before God?[4]
Will looking good always shadow doing good?

Oh, for a washing to wash our façade
Wash me, wash me, wash me I pray
Turn me, turn me, turn my way
'Til charity, justice, and truth I find.

And passing by on this side too
The Samaritan's badge I wear as mine[5]
For Jesus's sake and in Jesus's name.
John B. (Jack) Duncan, 1996

[1] Matthew 25:40
[2] Revelation 3:17
[3] Matthew 6:1
[4] Matthew 6:5
[5] Luke 10:30